ANOTHER DEAD TEENAGER

By Mark Richard Zubro

The "Tom and Scott" Mysteries

A Simple Suburban Murder
Why Isn't Becky Twitchell Dead?
The Only Good Priest
The Principal Cause of Death
An Echo of Death

The "Paul Turner" Mysteries

Sorry Now?
Political Poison
Another Dead Teenager

ANOTHER DEAD TEENAGER

A

Paul

Turner

Mystery

• BY MARK RICHARD ZUBRO •

St. Martin's

Press

New York

Library of Congress Cataloging-in-Publication Data

Zubro, Mark Richard.
    Another dead teenager / Mark Richard Zubro.
        p.   cm.
    "A Paul Turner mystery."
    ISBN 0-312-13024-4
    I. Title
PS3576.U225A83   1995
813'.54—dc20   95-15232
                                                                          CIP

First Edition: August 1995

10   9   8   7   6   5   4   3   2   1

ACKNOWLEDGMENTS

For their kindness, patience, and assistance:
Rick Paul, Barb D'Amato,
Hugh Holton, Kathy Pakieser-Reed

O N E

Paul Turner typed his name at the bottom of the Daily Log, his last act in the paperwork for their latest case. He let out a long breath.

Buck Fenwick tossed his pen on the pile of paper he'd been plowing through all morning.

"You done?" Fenwick asked.

Turner rubbed two fists over tired eyes and shoved himself away from his desk. "Yeah," he muttered. He glanced around the squad room. "Where is everybody?"

"They've been at lunch for hours. Come on." Fenwick's ever-expanding bulk necessitated regular feeding and he did not appreciate being late for meals.

They'd been working all morning on reports that capped a brief but sensational investigation. A couple had claimed they'd come home to their luxury high-rise apartment on Lake Shore Drive and found their eighteen-year-old son shot six times. Since they were rich, white, and lived at a wealthy address, the press had done their best swarm-of-locusts imitation around the grief-stricken parents and harassed cops. They had described their family life as more perfect than a warm-fuzzy sitcom on television. Conversations with the dead boy's friends, however, revealed a bleak but all too familiar picture of a family out of control. The friends told about a kid who flew into violent rages in confrontations with his parents, a kid who spent inordinate amounts of mysteriously gotten money on drugs and parties. The parents dismissed the discrepancy in views of the family's life as "nonsense from drug addicts who weren't worthy of being our son's friends." What the parents couldn't do was cover up the lack of footprints in the pools of blood around the body and the absence of bloodstains on their clothes, which would have been expected if they'd approached the body. As a father Turner knew if he found either of his sons hurt or injured, he'd have rushed to his side and not stood at a distance waiting for the police to confirm horrific news. These two anomalies and the differing family portraits were the starting points in convincing Turner that the parents had killed the kid themselves. Presented with their lack of appropriate parental response and a lot less pressure than Turner would have thought necessary, the father had blurted out the truth. You always looked not only at what the suspects did do, but what they didn't do.

Turner and Fenwick could have walked the three blocks to Dearborn Street for lunch, but Fenwick insisted on using the car. "Why walk when you could drive?" was Fenwick's motto. As he drove, he easily managed to outpace most of the gusts of wind hurrying through the South Loop. Cool early autumn air had replaced yesterday's thunderstorms.

Aunt Millie's Bar and Grill had been popular with cops for years. They packed the place at mealtimes and before and after each shift change, but no matter what time of day or night or even what item was ordered, all the food on the menu seemed to come out as mounds of artery-clogging glop or—on a good day—something akin to stale heaps of crust. The noisy, dim, smoke-filled room was usually crammed with cops. The motley mix occasionally got flavored with a lost tourist or two, or a couple of brave or demented locals. Two mystery writers had wandered in once, trying to get information about detective work. Millie told them lies while the real cops grinned and guffawed behind them. Aunt Millie's was the last bastion of a grittier Chicago past in the recently upscale Printers Row area of the city.

Turner and Fenwick joined Harold Rodriguez, Dwayne Smythe, and Ashley Devonshire, three other cops from Area Ten, at a circular booth near the back of the restaurant.

After raucus greetings and orders given to a waitress in a rhinestone-studded apron, Fenwick asked Rodriguez, "Where's Carruthers?"

Randy Carruthers, curse of the day shift, was Rodriguez's partner.

"Do I care?" Rodriguez said. "Maybe he fell into the lake and drowned or he was kissing ass so hard he died in a gas attack. I can only hope something unpleasant happened to him. If I ever decide to kill somebody, my fondest wish is that they assign the case to Carruthers. I'd never be caught."

Ashley pointed to Turner, then Fenwick, and asked, "Did you guys really wrap up that Lake Shore Drive shooting last night?"

Both detectives nodded.

Dwayne, pink-cheeked, with short, brush-cut black hair and perfect teeth, and Ashley, an African-American woman with a pleasant smile and a melodious voice, were the newest additions to the Area Ten detective squad. Their newness did not prevent them from adopting the most blatant attitude of "been-there, done-that" Turner had ever run into. If you had a crime with ten dead bodies, they had one with eleven. If you'd worked eighteen hours, they'd worked nineteen. If you'd solved a case in ten hours, they could have done it in nine.

"Damn, you guys are good," Dwayne said. He reached over and twiddled Fenwick's tie. The older cop growled. "You guys are good, but Ashley and I are good and lucky. That's the combination you've got to have."

Ashley patted Fenwick's hand. "You're cute when you're angry."

"I don't see why you worked so hard on the case," Rodriguez said. "They did the world a favor. It was just another dead teenager. Not enough of those around."

"It was their own kid," Ashley said. "You see it all the time."

Turner knew the source of Rodriguez's sourness on teenagers. Of Rodriguez's four kids, two had been in jail by the age of sixteen, a third was saved from prison only because he could run faster than an overweight beat cop, and the fourth had run away six months ago. Rodriguez's being a cop had protected his kids from prosecution only a little and that only in the beginning. Turner liked Rodriguez, found him affable as a companion and more than competent as a cop. He couldn't imagine the home life that led to such misery.

"All kids are rotten," Rodriguez said.

"You still encouraging teenagers to hang out on street corners and join gangs?" Fenwick asked.

"Whenever I can. More chances to shoot each other that way." For a few more minutes Rodriguez continued on a tirade about how awful kids were while the others ate in silence. Turner tuned him out. He'd heard the litany of teenage sins and perversions innumerable times before.

As their mounds of grease—reputedly burgers this afternoon—were delivered, Fenwick's radio crackled. Fenwick put the portable next to his ear to listen. He moved the mouthpiece to his lips, gave a brief response, and said to Turner, "We gotta go. Grab your stuff."

Turner didn't ask questions. He threw money on the table, picked up his burger and plastic cup filled with coffee, and followed Fenwick out to the car.

Behind the wheel Fenwick said, "We got a dead body in an abandoned warehouse at Twentieth and Lumber Streets." Fenwick drove and ate while Turner balanced his drink against Fenwick's quick starts, rapid acceleration, sharp turns, and abrupt stops. If he had to drive five feet or five hundred miles, he pushed a car as fast as it would go, rarely bothering with what the terrain or road conditions would allow.

"Body will still be dead when we get there," Turner said around several bites of burger.

Fenwick grunted. Turner was mostly used to Fenwick's mad careening, but he didn't relish the idea of a lapful of hot coffee.

They hurried down Clark Street to 20th and turned west to cross the river. A blue and white squad car rested on the pavement in front of a building bounded by the Chicago River, Lumber Street, and 20th Street. Most of the windows were broken out of the five-story structure. Grimy maroon bricks made up the walls of the hopelessly dilapidated outer shell of the old factory. They grabbed flashlights and notebooks and strode toward a uniformed cop standing on the threshold.

"You guys won't believe it," the cop said.

Turner didn't recognize the officer, who was short, blond-haired, and slender, but he did recognize the trembling and excitement. Probably just out of the police academy and hadn't seen a dead body before. The guy was torn between the desire to gape and the urge to toss his lunch.

"How'd the call come in?" Fenwick growled.

The cop blinked. He said, "Huh?"

"Who found the body? Who called it in?"

"Some little kid playing where he wasn't supposed to. That's not the big thing."

"What is?" Fenwick asked.

"The dead guy is Ken Goldstein's son."

Fenwick glared at the guy a moment, then said, "It's still just a dead guy."

Fenwick's attitude was the right one, Turner knew, but still the Goldstein name would bring hordes of reporters. Ken Goldstein had been the coach of two college basketball national championship teams in his years at St. Basil's University in Frankfort, a far south suburb of Chicago. Moving on from there, it took him ten years to win two national basketball championships in the NBA. For several years his name had been almost as magical in Chicago

5

sports as Michael Jordan's. The press circus of the case they just finished would be nothing compared to the mobs around them now.

"How do you know it's Goldstein's son?" Turner asked.

"Driver's license and other stuff in his wallet," the blond said.

"You touched the body?" Fenwick snapped.

"Just for identification."

Fenwick snarled and growled, then said, "Just for nothing, you dumb-shit numb-nuts asshole!" Fenwick enjoyed teaching rookie cops a lesson and Turner let him shout on. The kid had to learn sometime. Fenwick pushed his nose an inch from the young cop's face. "Never touch anything! Never! Don't go near the scene! Just call the detectives and stay away!"

The blond turned pale and gulped. His voice squeaked, "Yes, sir."

"Don't they teach you guys anything at the academy?" Fenwick didn't wait for an answer. "You got a partner in there screwing things up?"

"Yes, no." The cop scratched his head in bewilderment. "He's in there."

"Stay out here." Fenwick jabbed a finger into the cop's chest to punctuate each sentence. "Keep everybody out of here. I don't care if the Police Superintendent, the mayor, and the pope show up. Nobody gets in unless they're from the Crime Lab or the Medical Examiner's office."

"Yes, sir." The blond gave them directions for finding the body inside.

Before entering, Turner and Fenwick examined the pavement for twenty feet on either side of the entrance. Nothing amid the urban destruction jumped up and said, "I'm a clue."

Turner glanced at the buildings across the street. More boarded-up old factories or warehouses. The one on the corner a hundred feet away was a burned-out hulk. "Not gonna be a lot of witnesses in the neighborhood," Turner said.

"Not much traffic either," Fenwick added.

Outside, the gusting wind had whipped autumn cold through

every tiny opening in their clothes. Inside, Turner felt the cool and damp cloying at his skin. Light from outdoors filtered through the broken windows from former offices along the west side of the building. Remnants of this glow then seeped into the corridor they were in. They flipped on their flashlights and shone them ahead, then tramped carefully down the center of the structure. Most of the floor and ceiling on this level were still intact. The walls were water-stained and the floorboards mushed under their feet.

"Place should've been torn down," Fenwick said.

"No signs of blood and gore or dead bodies here," Turner said.

The building smelled of mold, urine, and excrement. The detectives passed a bank of empty, gaping service elevators. They encountered the promised stairway at the far end of the passage. They let their flashlight beams linger on each step and railing.

They ascended the stairs, and following the blond's directions, walked down a corridor, past five openings, and turned right.

A frightened voice called, "Who's there?"

They identified themselves. Seconds later another cop, younger than the one downstairs, put a trembling face around a corner. "It's a little spooky up here," he said.

"Where's the victim?" Turner asked.

The cop pointed into the room he'd just left and stepped out into the hall.

The naked male body lay on its back ten feet from the entrance to the room. A broken-out window on the east wall let in oblique sunlight and a slight breeze. Shattered glass and rotting fast-food containers lay strewn across half the floor. The walls had turned gray and brown, with blotches of mold spreading from corners or crevices where the paint had first begun to peel. A heap of clothes was scattered in one corner.

Neither detective made a move to enter the room. They would make preliminary observations and begin their sketches of the scene from here. Then along with the Crime Lab they'd make a painstakingly careful entrance.

"Lot of blood," Fenwick said.

Great gouts and spurts of blood had sprayed halfway up the two walls nearest the body. Vast pools of dark red covered nearly half the floor. The Crime Lab would automatically check for footprints inadvertently left by the killer here, in the hall, and any likely place in the building. One set was readily visible. Probably the cop who checked the identification. The pool of blood could have covered any others, or the killer could have brought a second pair of shoes, showing lots of planning and premeditation. A killer who stopped to clean up his footprints suggested a cool hand.

Turner could make out a gaping hole in the left side of the corpse's head, the blood and brains smeared on the filth-encrusted wall behind him. "Bullet holes in the torso are at a funny angle," Turner said.

"Funny ha-ha or funny weird?" asked Fenwick. The two of them crouched together in the wide doorway.

"Kind of coming up out of the body," Turner said. "I've seen at least a hundred of these and I've never seen holes like that. These aren't like they exploded straight through, one side to the other, but as if they sort of popped up from inside."

Fenwick shone the flashlight on the boy's wrists and ankles. "Round abrasions? Probably tied with a rope." He flicked the light over the body. "Nice-looking kid," he said.

Turner eyed the corpse dispassionately. The face with lifeless eyes staring was undamaged, with a few flecks of red under the chin and bits of interior body parts caught at the throat. It was a handsome face. Both broad shoulders were intact and the parts of the abdomen still recognizable as such were flat and muscular.

"Around fifteen or sixteen?" Fenwick opined.

Turner recalled reading an article in the paper when Ken Goldstein's son won the state of Illinois tennis high school championship a few weeks ago. He told Fenwick what he remembered. He finished, "The paper had a picture of him with this real attractive girl in a cheerleader outfit."

Fenwick played his flashlight on the gaping eyes. "One dead stud muffin," he said.

They stood up and retreated back into the corridor. Fenwick began examining the hallway with his flashlight. He stooped and pointed at a dark smear. "Could be blood," he said.

"We need to get lots more light in here," Turner said.

Fenwick gave a grunt of agreement, then added, "Half the goddamn reporters in the country are going to be sniffing around this one."

Whenever possible, the Commander of Area Ten put Turner and Fenwick on the cases that could involve lots of publicity. He knew the two detectives wouldn't be stampeded into making an arrest, and that they had an over 95 percent conviction rate on those they did bust. The commander wanted seasoned veterans who could ride out a media feeding frenzy, and he had them in Turner and Fenwick.

They heard noise behind them and turned to see members of the Crime Lab. Turner and Fenwick began making sketches of the scene in their regulation blue folders. Turner drew the body, noting the wound sites he could see without shifting it. He'd add more sketches when the medical examiner turned the body over.

Three hours later they'd learned a couple of things. They confirmed that the Kenitkamette police, where the dead boy lived, had a missing person report on Jacob Goldstein, the famous coach's son, but they also had one on a friend of the teen's, Frank Douglas, son of a former Olympic track and field star.

Turner, Fenwick, a local beat cop, the medical examiner, and two members of the Crime Lab held a conference next to the broken-out window of the room where they'd found the body.

What they had so far was evidence of only one killer. The murder had taken place in this room. More lab tests were necessary to check for traces of sexual assault; the victim had fought against his bonds.

The M.E. said to Turner, "You were right about the funny angle of some of the wounds. Kid was shot up the ass at least twice. Bullets came up and out." He nodded at the Crime Lab tech. "Fluid tests will tell us a lot. Killer kept shooting him after he was dead."

Turner said, "So somehow the killer gets the drop on an athletic teenager and ties him up. Chooses this place because it's isolated and abandoned so he won't be disturbed. Obviously picked out carefully."

"Homeless and gangs don't usually hang out in here," the local uniformed patrolman said. "It's too ruined even for them."

Turner said, "From the looks of this I'd say we've got a very angry person who is still able to plan extremely carefully."

Heads nodded.

The patrolman said, "I inventoried everything in the room. The kid's underwear is missing. I got jeans, socks, shoes, sweatshirt, undershirt, coat, but no shorts."

"Gosh, sounds like a clue to me," Fenwick said.

"Footprints you saw were definitely from the cop who identified him."

"Figures," Fenwick said.

"Who's the security firm for this place?" Turner asked.

The patrolman said, "Save-Our-Souls."

They all chuckled. Save-Our-Souls was their nickname for Illinois Safe Serve, the most notoriously useless security company in the area. Reputedly they hired retired suburban cops who were past the retirement age of any police department within hundreds of miles. Cop lore in the city had it that they gave their guards one bullet for their guns: If they had any trouble, they were supposed to shoot themselves. They were also the cheapest outfit in the city. Your insurance company, assuming you had one for some of these hulks, would see this wonderful firm on paper and assume you were a responsible landlord.

"We'll have to talk to the Kenitkamette police and find out where this kid was supposed to be," Fenwick said.

"Somebody was going to call," the patrolman said.

"I'll check in a minute," Turner said.

"We'll have to examine the outside of the building before we leave," Fenwick said. "We can probably get a couple of uniformed cops to go over it inch by inch."

"I don't envy you guys on this one," the M.E. said. "The dad was famous. So was the kid. You'll have people oozing out of the woodwork trying to 'help.' Ninety-nine point nine percent won't know shit."

"Maybe we'll even get a task force," Fenwick said.

"Gosh, shucks, I'm all excited," Turner said. He sighed. "I better go find that uniform with the report from Kenitkamette."

Turner reentered the room ten minutes later. "We have another call."

"Tell them we're going to interview the parents," Fenwick said. "They need to find somebody else."

"It's about the other kid. The one that was with Jake Goldstein."

"He's not sobbing his eyes out and confessing to murder, is he?" Fenwick asked.

"Not unless he's doing it from some kind of afterlife. They found him on the bottom level of the Columbus Drive parking garage. Single bullet hole through the head."

Fenwick glanced back at the shredded corpse in the room. "Killer used two different methods."

"Not that different," Turner said. "Gun in both cases. Maybe our killer just used one bullet there, but he had more time here. Or maybe the Douglas kid killed his buddy and then decided to blow himself away in an inconvenient parking garage."

"Or," Fenwick said, "a third person, maybe more, that we don't know about was on the scene, and killed them in different locations for obscure mystical reasons."

"Mystical?"

"It's my day of the month to be philosophical."

"I've been holding my breath for this moment."

"Why were they in town?"

"Bears game last night."

"Never understood that Thursday night shit."

"One of those cable television deals. Had them for a couple years now."

Fenwick glanced back at the room. "I guess we'll know more at the other scene."

In the Chicago Police Department, whoever got the first call on a case investigated all subsequent crimes discovered that had connection to the first. That meant Turner and Fenwick had another body. Not a chance they'd be home before midnight.

The uniform who had met them at the front door entered the room. "You guys might need to look at this place we found."

They followed him out the door.

"I shouldn't have snapped at you earlier," Fenwick said to the young cop. "Sorry."

The uniform shrugged.

Up a flight of stairs to the third floor at the far end of a hall, they found a room slightly smaller than the one with the dead body. The young cop pointed at a tattered sleeping bag, six pop cans, and boxes and wrappers for McDonald's burgers and French fries.

"What is this shit?" Fenwick asked. "Somebody said gangs and the homeless didn't show up here."

"Kids," the patrolman said. "Maybe the ones who found the body."

"Sweep it for everything, bag it all, and save it," Turner said. "Better have all the prints taken. Any other signs of habitation in the building?"

"This is all we found so far. We're taking a second look."

Before they got in their car, they walked slowly around the north, west, and south sides of the building. The fourth side formed part of the retaining wall for the Chicago River.

"Must have parked somewhere," Fenwick said. "Unless they drove up in a boat."

They craned their necks around the northeast corner of the building. The wall of the factory plunged straight down into the river. What might at one time have been a loading dock had long since been bricked over.

"No place to tie up or get in," Turner said.

The north side of the building had the entrance Turner and Fenwick had used. Rusting wire mesh covered the windows on the ground floor that faced Lumber Street on the west side of the building. A gangway barely wide enough for a person to walk through ran along half of the south side of the building. The other half faced a field overgrown with years of debris, weeds, and bushes.

"Hard to get in anywhere back here," Turner said.

"Stopping in front risks somebody driving by on the street."

They scrambled up the cracked concrete of the loading dock, which ran for the same length the field did. Any of several broken doors and smashed windows could have given the killer access.

"Better get all these dusted," Fenwick said.

"Hard to drag a squirming kid through here," Turner said.

"Must have done something. Let's get some uniforms to go over every inch of this."

Fenwick didn't even bother trying to take surface streets across the Loop. It was after four and it could take them over an hour to make a ten-minute trip through the rush-hour crush. Fenwick eased down Wells Street and took the cutoff to Lower Wacker Drive. They sped quickly along the road which ran between the Chicago River and the bottoms of decrepit buildings, whose nooks, crannies, and shadows housed a large portion of homeless hunkering down against the coming winter.

The group of people at the Wacker Drive entrance to the parking garage parted slowly to let the unmarked police car inch its way forward. While Fenwick waited for a uniformed male cop to unhook the Police Crime Scene tape, a young female cop leaned in the passenger-side window next to Turner and said, "Down on level three."

The tires squealed as Fenwick raced through the turns.

"Body's not going anywhere," Turner said.

Fenwick grunted.

On level three a small crowd of civilians stood near the lighted cashier's booth. A uniformed cop waved them over. He pointed around a wall that divided the sections of the garage. "That way."

"Who's down there?" Fenwick asked.

"Couple guys from Eleventh and State."

"Double fuck," Fenwick said.

Turner saw a knot of police brass and a few uniformed cops gathered about fifty feet beyond the curve to the next level. Among them Turner recognized the director of Research and Development, the commander of the Communication Division, and the deputy superintendent of Technical Services. They slouched and stared at something on the far side of a Chevrolet conversion van. They weren't going to contribute anything to the investigation. They were only deskbound cops come to gawk at the famous dead.

Keeping in mind Fenwick's dislike for brass and his ability to shoot his mouth off at the wrong moment, Turner made sure he got to the scene before Fenwick could make insistent comments about them butting out. "Could you all step over here for a minute?" Turner asked. "We need to make a few sketches."

The brass ambled a few feet away. Making preliminary sketches was a good excuse to get the brass to move and better than Fenwick bellowing at them to move their butts.

The Columbus Drive underground garage had only recently opened. The lines marking the parking spaces still gleamed bright yellow in their newness. The gray cinder blocks in their thousands held up tons of darker gray poured concrete. The neon lights interrupted and intruded upon the shadows, but seemed more to be in an armed truce with the darkness than conquering the night.

The body lay between the front of the van and the wall. Shadows hid nearly everything but the outline of a human form. Turner could barely make out the gaping hole in the left side of Frank Douglas's head. A shaft of light a few feet behind and above caught smears of blood and brains on the cement wall behind him. The feeble light managed to catch the white of the lifeless eyes. Even after so many years on the job, the open, staring eyes of death caused Turner to pause.

T W O

Twenty years earlier Frank Douglas's dad, Andy, had won gold medals in track and field at the Olympics. Turner recalled reading that Frank, eagerly following in his father's footsteps, won three heats at the state track meet late last spring.

Turner motioned over a blue-uniformed cop. "Who found him?"

"I did." He was overweight, sporting a graying mustache and the hairiest knuckles Turner ever saw.

"What happened?"

"Didn't see a gun. Didn't hear anything. Drove down here for a routine check. This underground parking garage is less than a month old and seldom filled. The van could have been here all night."

Turner glanced around the deserted area of the parking garage. Maybe the cop came down for a quick nap.

"Body wasn't visible from any angle. I saw the vehicle sitting by itself when I pulled through first thing this morning. Couple rumors around that drug guys use this area for deals now and then. I haven't seen any. When the van hadn't moved by this afternoon, I called it in and checked it out."

"How'd you know to have someone contact us?"

The overweight cop said, "It's been on the police radio about the Goldstein kid and that his buddy was missing."

"That tears it," Fenwick said. "One of the overzealous cops at the first scene decided to make a friend of a reporter. You can bet one of them already told the parents. Goddamn reporters suck on those scanners like a teenage boy on his first tit. Someone wanted to be able to tell the parents the bad news and get the scoop of a lifetime."

"That's how they found out about the van," the blue-uniformed cop said. "That was on the radio, too."

"Glad somebody told us," Fenwick said.

"Do you think I'll get to meet Coach Goldstein?" the cop asked.

Turner and Fenwick assigned him to get a list of all the police personnel who were there, when they got there, and who called them. In short order the Crime Lab van pulled up and the medical examiner put in his appearance.

A whole lot of police personnel, some the same as on Lumber Street, showed up to perform their ritual dance at a death scene. Turner ordered every inch of pavement on the entire floor of this level of the parking garage vacuumed on the off-chance a microscopic piece of the criminal had been left behind. The youngest guy on the Crime Lab van groaned as he started the Augean task.

In his notebook Turner began drawing the crime scene, placement of the body, the van, and any other detail he observed.

They took pictures. Every inch of the interior and exterior of the van was dusted for fingerprints. After the fingerprinting and vacuuming of the van were done, Turner and Fenwick turned every knob, probed every crevice, opened, looked under, and did everything short of rip up the seat cushions, which might be done

1 6

later after their exterior was examined for microscopic traces of anyone who might have been in the van.

They found and catalogued a set of golf clubs missing the putter, a Chicago Cubs baseball hat, three different brands of tennis racquets, the spare tire and equipment for changing it, a condom still in its foil packet stuck in the folds of the back seat, but no gun and no hint about the murderer or why these boys died.

Three hours later Turner, Fenwick, and the forensic experts, the M.E., and members of the Crime Lab huddled twenty feet from the van.

"What've we got for sure?" Fenwick asked.

The M.E. said, "Kid got blasted where he fell. Probably dead before he hit the pavement. No blood inside the van. Won't know if the other kid's blood was here until we get test results back, but my opinion is, we won't find any of Goldstein's. This blood came from this kid. Probably the same caliber of gun both places—tests will tell us for sure."

"No sign of a struggle here," Fenwick said. "Could this one have killed the other and then come back here and shot himself?"

Turner asked, "If they parked here for the game, why come back here to off yourself, and if he killed himself, where's the gun?"

A young Crime Lab tech said, "Gun could have been stolen. Somebody homeless, gangbanger, whatever, sees it, takes it. Free gun that can't be traced to the taker."

"We'll have to find if they had access to guns," Turner said.

The M.E. said, "Can't rule out homicide and then suicide, but do you really believe a bum-takes-the-gun deal here?"

"I don't," Fenwick said. "Wallet with fifty bucks in this kid's back pocket. Rolex still on his wrist. Didn't rob the other kid, either. I think it's a double murder."

Heads nodded.

"Mob hit, drugs?" the Crime Lab tech asked.

Turner said, "They'll check the van for traces of commonly

controlled substances. No booze around. We didn't find anything suspicious in the van."

Another Crime Lab tech opined, "Kids this age getting shot. Gotta be drugs or gangs."

"Kids like this don't do drugs."

They all stared at the youthful member of the Crime Lab unit who had made this comment. "What'd I say? These guys were athletes. Their dads are famous."

"Who is this guy?" Fenwick asked. "You take stupid pills or does it come naturally?"

The guy turned red.

The M.E. said, "Is this the if-you're-an-athlete-you're-a-saint theory of police work?"

"Why don't you go help your buddy vacuum?" Fenwick said. The young guy shuffled off.

Turner said, "Whoever shot the Goldstein kid was really angry. You don't fire that many shots into somebody unless you're completely out of control. This one looks like it might have been impulse. One shot, real quick, get out. Lots of danger of somebody driving through."

"Why these kids?" Fenwick asked. No one had an answer, but often major hints to the killer came from figuring out why he or she had picked these victims.

"We've got to move on talking to the parents," Turner said. The meeting broke up.

The blue-uniformed cop they'd met on first entering this level gave them the paperwork he'd compiled. "You going to meet the coach?"

Turner nodded.

"I heard from one of the reporters upstairs. The families know their kids are dead," the cop said. "Reporters told them. Both sets of parents are at the Goldsteins waiting for news. Cops from Kenitkamette are at the house with them now. Think it's the Chief of Police. Said they'd wait for you."

"How do they know all this?" Fenwick asked.

"Cops called down here. Everybody wants to be part of this," the blue-uniformed cop said. "This is one of the biggest murders ever in Chicago."

"How lucky for us," Fenwick said.

It was just after eight when Turner and Fenwick started for Kenitkamette to talk to the parents. They took the newly reconstructed Kennedy Expressway to the Edens. Rush hour was over, but Fenwick managed to use most of his kamikaze tactics on the way up. They exited east on Lake Cook Road and picked up Sheridan Road into the exclusive North Shore suburbs. In Kenitkamette no home cost less than five hundred thousand to build and no lot was less than ten acres.

Using their Rand McNally *Chicago & Vicinity 6 County Street Finder,* they located the Goldsteins' address at the end of a long, winding drive called Crescent Lane. The two Chicago cops took in the circular drive with a Rolls-Royce and a Bentley parked amid a scattering of Kenitkamette police cars.

Fenwick glanced at the vast expanse of the house behind a porticoed front porch that ran the length of the building. "My entire year's salary couldn't pay for this front porch or for me to live on it," he said.

"They'll let us walk on it," Turner said.

A butler with wispy gray hair and a face crisscrossed with age lines opened the door before they could knock. He ushered them silently down a hall with a pale purple marble floor adorned only with three chairs set equidistant from each other. Turner had never seen the like. One chair was made of horseshoes and a tractor seat, another of black steel tubing and wood, and a third was adorned with kitchen utensils.

Fenwick said, "I've got chairs as junky as that in my house."

"Yeah, but yours came from Kmart. I bet these cost a fortune."

They entered what Turner guessed was a living room. At the far end, before the gaping maw of an enormous, unlit fireplace, they met Mr. and Mrs. Goldstein, the Douglases, and the entire upper echelon of the Kenitkamette Police Department: three women and two men, the one of highest rank being Donna Robsart, chief of police.

Coach Goldstein and Mr. Douglas looked pretty much like the pictures in the paper Turner remembered. Goldstein did have a lot less hair than in his photos and his paunch protruded less than on television. He stood next to his wife, who was seated on a low-arm sofa with a cream denim slipcover. She wore blue linen trousers and a white silk blouse. Facing the Goldsteins, Andy Douglas and his wife sat next to each other on an oversized sofa with a cotton slipcover and two needlepoint throw pillows. His hair was much whiter than Turner remembered seeing. She wore her hair pulled back severely to emphasize high cheekbones and violet eyes. The Douglases held hands.

After introductions and being seated, Mr. Douglas said, "All these reporters. All this confusion." He paused and sucked in a breath. "Is it really true?"

"I'm sorry," Turner said. "Yes, both boys are dead."

Mrs. Douglas buried her face on her husband's shoulder. They wept together. Mr. Goldstein abruptly sat on the edge of the couch next to his wife and with one hand he patted her shoulder while with the other he brushed futilely at the tears pouring down his cheeks. Mrs. Goldstein pulled a tissue from a box next to her and held it to her face. This was the confirmation of their worst fears.

When sufficient equilibrium returned and all of the local police except the chief had left, Turner said, "We need to ask you a few questions. Any details you can remember could be useful. It also might help if we could look at each boy's room."

What the parents knew of the previous evening was simple enough. The boys had gone to the football game the night before. They had access to a sky box as well as sideline passes secured by Mr. Goldstein. Afterward they were to have been escorted to the locker room to talk to a few of the players. The parents expected the boys home around one in the morning.

"It was late for a school night," Mr. Goldstein said, "but it was a rare opportunity. I'd have gone with them, but I had a speaking engagement in Kenosha. My wife and I arrived home around eleven-thirty."

Mr. Douglas said, "We were at a fund-raising dinner and meeting for Special Needs kids. We got home a little after midnight."

"They were so eager to go," Mrs. Goldstein said. "They'd been talking about it for weeks."

When their son Jake hadn't called or gotten in by two, they called the Douglases. By three they'd phoned the police. Their status and wealth got them more than a let's-wait-and-see from the local cops and a missing persons report was filed by seven in the morning.

"What happened to them?" Mr. Goldstein asked.

Turner gave them the bare facts of the case, leaving out the grimmer details both because he didn't want to upset them further, but also because, grief-stricken as these people might be, they could be suspects, and he didn't want to give the murderer any information he or she might find useful.

When Turner finished, Mrs. Goldstein said, "We'll do everything we can to help find the killer." The other parents nodded agreement.

"Any enemies, fights, break-up with girlfriends, new girlfriends with disgruntled old boyfriends?" Fenwick asked.

None of the parents knew of any such problem.

"Both of the boys were popular at school," Mrs. Douglas said. "They had lots of friends. They'd known each other since eighth grade. Did lots of things together."

"Any family problems, drugs, drinking?" Fenwick asked.

Turner watched the four parents carefully. When the personal questions started, emotional explosions could occur.

"We talked about that a little bit before you came," Mrs. Douglas said. "To see if something in either home could have been part of this. None of us could think of anything. I can't imagine something at home causing this." The other parents agreed with her.

"None of you left after you came home?" Turner asked.

Hints of anger and resentment flashed on their faces at the question, but the four of them muttered no or shook their heads.

"Did they have access to guns?" Fenwick asked.

As far as either set of parents knew, neither boy had ever fired a gun or even touched one.

The chief of police said, "We know who the troublemakers are in this town. Believe me, it was not these two boys. They were great. Lots of good press in the papers. Did lots of work in the community. Helped deaf kids every Saturday morning at the Methodist church. Nice kids. Wouldn't hurt anybody."

They were told that Jake Goldstein had an older brother who was a Rhodes Scholar in England. Frank Douglas had an older married sister living in Australia.

Turner and Fenwick gave them assurances that all would be done to find the killer or killers.

They examined the Goldstein boy's room before they left. Ken Goldstein accompanied them to the door.

"Mr. Goldstein," Turner said, "I need to ask. Did your son wear underwear all the time?"

"I beg your pardon."

"When we found him, we found a set of clothes with everything except shorts."

"I can't believe he was naked. He'd fight. He'd never take his clothes off for some pervert."

"He might not have had a choice, Mr. Goldstein. It would help if you knew if he wore underwear all the time."

"I presume he did. Doesn't everyone? He's bought his own clothes for quite some time. I honestly don't know for sure, but he must have."

"Thank you, sir."

Mr. Goldstein watched them enter his son's room. "I don't need to stay, do I? I'd rather be with my wife."

"No problem, sir."

"You'll be careful?" He looked over the room and tears started flowing.

"We'll be very gentle, Mr. Goldstein."

After Mr. Goldstein left and they stepped onto the plush gold floor covering, Fenwick said, "Nice carpet. Got his own john too." They peered into the medicine cabinet. "Somehow I knew we wouldn't find illegal drugs," Fenwick said. "I hate it when murder victims are saints."

There was toothpaste, aspirin, muscle-relaxing cream, deodorant, hair spray, zit cream, nail clippers, and a brush and comb set. Turner pointed at the pimple medicine. "At least he got zits."

"Do saints get zits?" Fenwick asked.

The faucets were gold-plated, the tile expensive, the porcelain gleamed. No hints of cause for murder.

The bedroom itself had a dresser, chest of drawers, and a king-size bed. A bookcase along one wall had textbooks neatly lined up on the top shelf with a variety of trophies and photos of teams resting on the other shelves. Turner glanced at these. It looked like the pictures Turner had of his older son. Goldstein's started from when the boy must have been nine or ten. The wall over the bed had a life-sized poster of Michael Jordan. On the opposite wall was an eight-foot picture of a Porsche.

Turner and Fenwick stood at the desk next to the bookcase. Fenwick glanced around the room. "This place is too neat. Who ever heard of a kid not leaving underwear around and crap all over?"

"The maid probably cleans it," Turner said.

"Maids clean underwear?"

In the dresser they found a drawer with rows of briefs and T-shirts neatly lined up.

"Had underwear," Fenwick said.

They looked in the closet. Clothes hung neatly, shoes arranged carefully, athletic equipment stored in individual open shelving.

They opened each container. In a black Chicago White Sox gym bag on the bottom shelf Fenwick found three neatly folded jockstraps, two Kenitkamette High School jerseys that had been ironed, a leather jockstrap, metal-studded belt and armband, plus one black and one pink dildo.

Fenwick gathered up the last five items in his arms. "These are a little different for a high school kid."

"I hope so," Turner said. Turner found a similar gym bag tucked further into the corner from which they'd grabbed the other. He opened it. "Fascinating. We've got a whip, chains, tit clamps, an electric butt plug, and several smaller dildos."

"This is really an electric butt plug?" Fenwick asked.

"Yeah."

"How do you know?"

"Doesn't every well-equipped S and M dungeon have several?"

"I guess. Wonder if Mom and Dad know about all this?"

"Bet not. I know Brian buys his own clothes and stuff, but I can't imagine him even knowing where to get this kind of material."

"Do you?"

"Well, yeah."

"If adults can find it, kids can too."

"These don't mean much by themselves," Turner said.

Fenwick examined under the bed and between the mattress and box spring. "No dirty books hidden away."

"You won't be able to add to your collection."

"He's got to whack off to something."

"Saints beat off?"

"Probably not athlete saints," Fenwick said.

They examined each drawer of the desk as they had the other pieces of furniture. Nothing indicated anything out of the ordinary. The simplicity and neatness made it easy for them to finish in less than half an hour.

Before leaving the house, they got a list of friends and teachers from the parents. From Donna Robsart they got a promise of cooperation and a commitment of personnel for the next morning for interviews at the high school. Turner and Fenwick told her they didn't want to wait until Monday to question people. Robsart promised to have available as many of the friends, teachers, coaches, and administrators as possible for a Saturday. Turner and

Fenwick asked them to include acquaintances and those who knew the boys only slightly.

When conducting interviews of people who knew the deceased in a murder case, the police liked to start with those who knew the victims least. People on the periphery of the victims' lives were the ones most likely to know the negative rumor, harbor ill will, know the tawdry gossip that might lead to a clue, a break in the case, or a conviction. They rarely started with those who knew the dead person best. Those are mostly people who liked the dead person, and only have good things to say. The Kenitkamette police would try to do this screening before the Chicago cops returned in the morning.

They followed the Douglases' car to their home to inspect Frank's room. All Turner could see as the gleam of the headlights raced across the front of the house was that it had a heavily beamed Tudor exterior. Mrs. Douglas led them up beige-carpeted stairs to her son's room. She opened the door and brought them in.

"I'm sorry it's such a mess." She stooped to begin picking up clothes from the floor.

"Please, stop, Mrs. Douglas," Turner said gently. "We'd rather just look at it as is."

She halted and then said, "You won't hurt anything?"

"We're just trying to get hints about him that could help us solve the murder."

"I can't imagine what you'd find here that could lead to the killer. He was such a good boy. Surely you won't find anything. . . ." Her voice trailed off. She nodded uncertainly and stood in the doorway observing their work.

Her presence limited the commentary between the two detectives.

The room had sports posters of tennis and track players on three walls. A king-size bed, a chest of drawers, a dresser, and a desk. This room had mounds of dirty clothes on the floor with whiffs of rotting jockstrap emanating from several of them. Five or six pairs of shoes were piled in one corner. The desk chair was hung with jumbled dress pants and shirts. The closet was a mass of athletic equipment draped over, under, and around a myriad of shirts, pants, and jackets, some on hangers, some thrown carelessly about.

Turner checked the scattering of school books on top of the desk, in the center of which was a pad of paper with an opening paragraph of an essay about the castles of Europe. It would never be finished. The center drawer, positioned over the space where one could sit, was filled with more paper, pens, pencils, stamps, and envelopes. The first drawer on the right had old gym locks, assorted keys, a condom, a harmonica, a police whistle on a string, and heaps of similar paraphernalia, but no clues to murder. The second drawer had papers from past school years. The bottom drawer had more paper on top but near the bottom was a magazine with pictures of naked women. Under that was a notebook.

Turner opened it and then beckoned Fenwick over. The two detectives paged slowly through the three-ring notebook.

"What is it?" Mrs. Douglas asked. She moved across the room toward them.

Turner showed her the first several pages.

"I don't understand."

"This is the Satanic alphabet. Someone was practicing the letters."

"My son wouldn't be involved in any of that nonsense."

"He wasn't?"

"Most definitely not."

She could add herself to the long list of parents who weren't aware of what their kids were doing.

"We'd like to take this with us," Turner said.

"Certainly. I wouldn't want it in the house."

They left. Fenwick took the same route back to the city. As they drove through the Kennedy/Edens junction, he said, "Parents claim their kids were saints. Sex toys and Satanism don't seem to mix with the image of a saintly teenager."

"You can't expect much different from parents at a time like this," Turner said, "and parents don't know a lot of things about their kids. There's stuff about Brian I'm sure I'd rather not know. I did stuff as a kid I hope my parents never find out about."

"Like what?"

"Same stuff you did, probably. Want to tell me about it?"

Fenwick thought a minute. "You're right," he said.

Turner said, "I just hope tomorrow when we talk to the friends and teachers, we'll get some lead. Somebody must know something about sex toys and Satanism."

"And if it's got anything to do with the murders."

It was just after midnight when they got back to Area Ten headquarters. Even at this late hour three reporters from radio stations and two from newspapers along with a television crew were waiting for them outside. They ran this gauntlet and then had to answer to the commander, the case sergeant, and the chief of detectives for over an hour. No one had any ideas for actions they should take beyond what had been examined and who had been questioned so far. They discussed the probability of pressure from press, public, and parents and how to deal with it. They outlined strategies for the morning.

On the way to their desks they passed Joe Roosevelt and Judy Wilson, two detectives from the squad. Joe was red-nosed and short, with brush-cut gray hair and bad teeth. Judy was a fiercely competitive African-American woman. They had a well-deserved reputation as one of the most successful pairs of detectives on the force. They were arguing with the watch commander outside an interrogation room. Their heated debate was about the necessity or lack thereof for giving a suspect they'd been questioning for three hours his *Miranda* warning. The difference between a probable suspect and an actual suspect can be subtle. Roosevelt said, "He was a witness until he started talking about the gun."

"But did he say it was his gun?" Wilson asked.

"I thought he said. . . ."

Turner and Fenwick left them to it. They sat at their desks for almost two hours to begin the detailed paperwork that a police bureaucracy requires.

They knew they would have to be extra careful to cover

themselves. Every reporter in the city would be after them for details, but more important, everyone in the brass would be looking over their shoulders to make sure they'd pursued every lead as far as it would go and that every case file was completed absolutely correctly. Too much of what they wrote on many cases was simply to cover their asses. Turner and Fenwick had been detectives long enough that doing everything correctly was almost intuitive. They'd have to go by instinct and then double- and triple-check everything. Careers could be lost with a screw-up on a case like this. The pressure would be intense to solve it quickly and be right.

Turner left for home just before three. More nights than he cared to remember they'd been required to stay all night to work on a case. In this instance there were no leads to follow, suspects to question, witnesses on hand to interrogate, or vital information to be hunted for. They'd only gotten the essentials of the paperwork done before calling it a night. They'd have to start early in the morning on more interviews and examination of possible evidence, all of which would add to the mounds of forms to be completed.

T H R E E

Through his front window Paul Turner could see Ian Hume's six-foot six-inch frame sprawled in the golden brown easy chair. One leg swung over an arm of the chair and another stretched out onto a red, velvet-covered ottoman. Ian's slouch fedora was low over his eyes. Turner saw him reach a hand up and scratch the front of his beard-bedecked chin, a sure sign that Ian was immersed in the book he was reading. Turner saw that it was a hardcover edition of *Conduct Unbecoming* by Randy Shilts.

Ian was the star reporter for the city's major gay newspaper, the *Gay Tribune*. Several years before, he'd won the Pulitzer Prize for investigative journalism for his exposé of the medical establishment's price-fixing of AIDS drugs.

Paul and Ian had gone through the police academy together and after graduation had been assigned to the same district as beat cops. They'd come to respect and like each other, but Ian had gotten fed up with the system, and in addition made the decision to come out. He'd gone back for his journalism degree and begun writing newspaper articles; then he'd quit the department to work full time as a reporter for the local gay newspaper. Ian had been a great help to Paul in the emotionally difficult time after his wife's death, when Jeff was born. They had been lovers for three years and close friends since. Occasionally they had been of some help to each other on cases.

Paul unlocked his front door and stepped in. Ian used one finger to raise the brim of his hat an inch to look at Paul. "You're late," Ian said.

"I know baby-sitting is one of your favorite things," Paul said. "I wanted you to get as much time in as possible."

"It's a joy in my life right up there with being tortured to death by crazed terrorists."

"You've never been tortured by anybody."

"Maybe I'll get lucky."

Paul sat on the edge of the worn brown couch. The arms were threadbare where years of legs had been draped while lounging. "Is Jeff asleep?"

"You need to speak to that child," Ian said.

Paul raised an eyebrow. "He beat you at which game tonight?"

"All of them, including chess for the first time. I know he's your kid and all, but at the age of eleven he's a menace. And he showed me how to do several things with my laptop computer that no one below the age of thirty should be able to do."

"Serves you right for asking."

"It was a delight when I insisted he had to go to bed. At least when he's asleep I've got a chance of winning."

"I don't hear loud annoying music from downstairs," Paul said. "What's happening with the team?" Paul's older son, Brian, had invited over more than a dozen members of his high school football team to spend the night.

"They were watching some movie earlier," Ian said. "It was filled with guns and violence and studly men. I was not invited to watch. They might have another one. The only part of the conversation I was able to overhear concerned the physical attributes of the female of the species."

Paul rose and walked into the kitchen. Ian followed. As they passed the door open to the basement, they could hear the sound of male voices.

Paul took a bottle of orange juice out of the refrigerator, found a glass, and poured himself some.

Ian glanced down the stairs and then moved close enough to whisper in Paul's ear, "I want to know who the one is in the white jeans and black T-shirt. He drove up here on a crotch rocket."

Paul grinned at his friend. "Do I want to know what that is?"

"It's a Ducati, a motorcycle, one of the most expensive made. It is an exotic Italian racing bike. It's got fully integrated. . . ."

"I've got the idea. The bike and the kid are sexy."

"The kid walked in here with Oakley Blade sunglasses, the ones with a blue-mirrored surface? It was hours after sunset. He also wore a black leather jacket that made him look more butch than the entire clientele of a leather bar on a Saturday night, and I have never seen anybody that sexy in white jeans."

"I'm not going down there on an inspection tour for you. I did see a motorcycle parked in front of the neighbors'. Why didn't you just introduce yourself?"

"I tried to get Brian to introduce me to all of them. He told me they were all straight and that I wouldn't have any luck with any of them."

"Need I remind you that they are all below the age of eighteen, and every one of them is jail bait?"

"I do not diddle little boys," Ian said severely. "Anyway, some of them downstairs are bigger than I am. Need I also point out that I had sex for the first time when I was thirteen. It was with a nineteen-year-old male prostitute in Omaha, Nebraska, and I want you to know. . . ."

"I've heard the story," Paul said. "I know you're proud of being a sexual athlete from an early age, but I have no quarrel with the age-of-consent laws and the crowd underneath us isn't fair game for you yet."

"I can wait, and I can look, and I can have lust in my heart. Besides, you're the one who invited me here to baby-sit."

"I did not 'invite' you to baby-sit. Only because Ben's visiting his family and Mrs. Talucci hasn't been feeling well are you here."

Ben Vargas was the man Paul had been dating for over a year.

"What's wrong with Rose?" Ian asked.

"I'm not sure," Paul said. "I'm a little worried."

"She'll tell you when she's ready," Ian said.

Rose Talucci lived next door to Paul Turner. She had the ground floor of the house to herself. On the second floor lived Mrs. Talucci's two daughters and several distant female cousins. At ninety-two Mrs. Talucci ruled this brood, her main concern being to keep them out of her way and to stay independent. Numerous times she'd confided in Paul that if they weren't family, she'd throw them all out. She did her own cooking, cleaning, and shopping, as she had for seventy-four years. To her daughters' horror, she took the bus on her own throughout the city and even to suburbs to visit friends, relatives, attend shopping-center openings, or anything else that struck her fancy. Paul loved Rose. She cared for Jeff after school whenever Paul or Brian couldn't be home, and often wound up giving the boys and their dad dinner. This was prearranged on a weekly basis. For several years after it started, she refused all offers of payment. Being neighbors and nearly family precluded even discussing such things. But one day Mrs. Talucci couldn't fix a broken porch. Paul had offered, and since then he'd done all repairs and had even made several major renovations on her home. Her being ill was unheard of, but she hadn't been willing to tell him about it yet. Paul planned to talk with her again in the morning.

"Why do you need someone to watch these kids anyway?" Ian asked. "They're all old enough to take care of themselves. It's not as if they were going to try making out with each other, although that is not a bad concept."

"I didn't want Brian to have to be responsible for Jeff. Brian had enough to do with taking care of the party. As for the teens in the basement, you put fifteen high school kids together and I, for one, want them to have in their heads somewhere that there is an adult within reasonable proximity. I don't think Brian and his friends would do anything, but you've got to remember kids will act like kids most of the time, not like Supreme Court Justices."

"Are they going to sleep in their underwear?" Ian asked.

"The Supreme Court Justices?"

Ian glared. "I was referring to the undergarments of the crowd in the basement."

"They all brought sleeping bags. I presume they're going to sleep in them. Clothed, unclothed, or somewhere in between, I have no idea nor do I have any interest. I'm sure they'll manage."

"Is it normal for high school boys to have sleepovers? I thought girls did it and called them slumber parties?"

"Don't be sexist," Paul said. "Most of these guys have been on the same team at the same high school for three or four years. Sometimes they go out on dates or go to the movies before they go to somebody's house to hang out."

"Sounds odd to me," Ian said. "Maybe one of them needs an older, wiser man to explain the ways of the world to him, or perhaps a group lecture would be helpful."

"Why didn't you suggest that to them earlier before I got home?" Paul asked.

Ian ignored him. "I bet every one of them is wearing tight white Jockey shorts even as we speak."

"I suppose," Turner said. "How much have they eaten?"

"An inordinate amount of pizzas were delivered about three hours ago. I think the food lasted all of fifteen seconds. An hour after inhaling everything but the carpet, they sent one of their number to the store. He came back with a car full of snacks."

"They didn't sneak any liquor in?" Paul asked.

"I hope so. Maybe one of them will get drunk and need an older, wiser man to care for him until the effects of demon rum have worn off."

"Why don't you take your older, wiser ass out of here? I can handle it from this point."

Ian sniffed. "You just want to hog them all to yourself."

"You're welcome to approach any of them," Paul said. "I'm sure each of them would have a unique response to any proposition from you."

"Thanks for the useless invitation. I'd probably be beaten and raped over and over again, and I don't have time for that tonight."

"Being raped by teen-aged boys is not a fantasy that many in this society would relish or approve of," Paul said.

Ian stood up. "That's their problem. I've always thought being ravished by a football team would be a delight, although I would prefer a college crowd. I'm no fool, I wouldn't touch the little darlings downstairs."

"You wouldn't want to stay the night? I need a keeper for them for a short while in the morning. I've got to leave early for work."

"Sorry, I'm meeting the suicide woman from Washington State for lunch."

"Which one is this?"

Paul knew about Ian's pet project on teen suicide. Ian was convinced that many of the suicides reported were caused because the kids couldn't deal with their sexuality. He wanted to prove that gay teens were a large portion of both suicides and true runaway teens in this country. His problem was getting people to talk. Ian found it difficult to walk up to a grieving parent and ask, "Did your child kill himself/herself because they couldn't cope with being gay?"

"It was some sports hero. Hanged himself in the gymnasium the day before some big championship game. I managed to get the coroner to talk to me a little bit at the time. She's changing jobs and passing through Chicago."

"Didn't he die years ago?"

"I keep in contact with possible sources. I send them articles, little notes. She responded more than most. Sometimes I get lucky. At any rate, my teenage baby-sitting duty is done for the next decade."

"Good luck with your interview." Turner followed his friend to the front door. "Thank you for helping out and thank you for not letting your libido get the best of you."

Ian made his fingers on one hand into a circle and jerked it back and forth rapidly. "I'll wait until I get home. You get pictures of any of them, I get dibs, but at least find out the name of the kid in the white jeans. He will break hearts before he's through."

Paul looked in on his younger son, Jeff. The eleven-year-old slept on his side, breathing easily. He noted the leg braces on the floor and the catheterization equipment on the nightstand. Amid the debris was the scrapbook Jeff kept of his older brother's sports accomplishments. The recent newspaper article on Brian was askew on the top, waiting to be taped in place. This one had made the front page of the *Tribune*'s sports section. There had been pictures and a lengthy article about Brian and his best friend on the team, Jose. They'd been setting high school records as a quarterback and receiver combination.

Paul smoothed the covers and then sat on the edge of the bed. He watched his son sleep. Jeff had the birth defect spina bifida. That meant that at birth his spinal cord and nerves protruded in a sac from his back, near the bottom of his spine. He was born with bladder and bowel dysfunction and paralysis of his legs. Except for a brief scare a year before to unclog the shunt in Jeff's head, there had been no major health problems in recent years.

As Paul sat at his son's side, unbidden he began remembering the conversation he'd had with the grieving parents earlier. He saw them vividly in his mind. No good trying to block the remembrance. At the crime scene he could distance himself as a professional doing his job, but now this late at night with his younger son gently sleeping, the unwanted memory of the horrors crept from the corners of his mind. He let it flow through him for a few minutes, then shuddered involuntarily, trying to shake off the images. He touched Jeff's hair gently, patted him, and eased out of the room.

Paul returned to the kitchen and began cleaning up debris. Occasionally he heard snatches of conversation from the basement. He filled the sink with warm water and washed cups, glasses, and bowls. He'd do this much for Brian, but his older son would clean all remnants of the party from the basement tomorrow.

As he plunked the last bowl in a cupboard, he heard a deep voice from the basement complaining, "I'm not going to be eligible to play next week. I'm flunking English. I didn't get my book report in."

"You dumb shit," another voice said. "We need you. How could you be that stupid?"

The deep voice replied, "I tried to get to the store to rent the video, but by the time I got there it had been checked out."

"You ever think of reading the book, Fred?" Turner recognized his son Brian's voice.

"Read it? Jesus. Not when there's a video out."

"You dumb shit." This was an angry voice that Paul didn't recognize.

"Relax," a voice cooed. "It's no big deal." This was not Fred's deep voice.

Turner wasn't sure if the topic had changed or not. He felt only a twinge of guilt at listening in. The world of teenagers was a mystery to him, and he couldn't resist listening. In a minute he'd leave. Tired as he was, he'd sit up for a while reading the paper to make sure the boys downstairs were settled for the night. Then he'd make his way up to his own bed.

"Tom, get that crap out of here. His dad's a cop. He could come home at any minute."

Paul froze. The voices downstairs were silent for a moment.

"You guys get so hyper," the one who had urged them to relax said.

"Out!" Paul had seldom heard his older son sound so angry.

"You're kidding?"

"Out!" Brian repeated.

Paul debated casually walking downstairs. He knew most of the boys, and it wouldn't be odd for him to say hello.

Several seconds of silence passed.

"Now," Brian said. His voice was flat and even.

Paul heard rustling below. He quietly crept into the living room and sat in the easy chair. Half a minute later a hulking teen eased past him to the front door. Paul recognized him, but didn't remember his name. The teenager saw Paul and the boy's face turned gray as he hurried out the door.

Paul picked up a copy of today's paper and began to peruse it casually. Fifteen minutes later he heard voices in the kitchen.

He wandered in and saw two boys rummaging in the refrigerator. One was Brian, who wore a University of Wisconsin jersey top and the white warm-up pants with the St. Felicita's High School logo on the front left leg. Next to Brian was his best friend from the team and the other boy in the article, Jose Martin. Jose was always polite and friendly to Turner, but seldom said much. He was an inch shorter than Brian's six feet one and slightly thinner but he was one of the toughest football players Paul had ever seen. Jose could take incredible punishment from an entire defensive line and bounce back up again. His dusky gold skin reflected his Hispanic heritage.

Paul noted that Jose wore tight white jeans that required no belt for them to cling to his narrow hips and that emphasized his butt nicely. His black T-shirt completed the ensemble, so Paul assumed this was the kid Ian had mentioned. Paul shook his head. He recognized that Jose was good-looking, as was his own son for that matter, but he felt absolutely no stirring of desire. He'd always wanted to make love to a man, not a kid. He did see that Jose's plain black T-shirt tucked into his pants made more prominent the kid's broad shoulders tapering down to his narrow hips. Paul hadn't known the boy owned a motorcycle.

They exchanged greetings.

"Any problems with the party?" Paul asked.

"No," Brian said. "Everything's under control. Ian behaved himself."

"Good. Is that one of the guys' motorcycle out front?"

"Mine, Mr. Turner." Jose smiled with pride of ownership. "Of course, my dad had to put money down and sign for me. I've got to cover the cost of the insurance and every other payment."

Paul wasn't sure it was a great idea to get a seventeen-year-old a vehicle that expensive, but it wasn't his son. He'd never met Jose's dad and didn't know if he came to the games to watch his son. He was pleased that the boy had to be responsible for a large chunk of the cost.

"Good luck with it." Paul said to Brian, "I'm going to bed. You need anything, I'll be upstairs."

Brian mumbled thanks. He and his buddy hurried downstairs with what looked like last night's leftovers. Paul sighed and trudged up to his room.

Paul dragged himself out of bed at seven the next morning. In the shower he let hot water pour onto his tired face for five minutes in an attempt to revive himself. Originally he'd been scheduled to be off today, but with a case such as this, he knew it would be a full day. After he'd dressed and eased his way downstairs, he peered into Jeff's room and saw his younger son still asleep. He then listened at the door to the basement stairs. He heard a muffled snort and a mild snore, but no other noise from the boys gathered below.

He turned the automatic coffee maker on, poured some tomato juice in a glass, and leaned against the counter. Tired as he was now, he knew it would only get worse if the case wasn't solved in a short time.

A normal Saturday would find Paul involved with his sons in household chores, with Brian trying to sleep through them all and Jeff attempting to play computer games instead of working. After the morning squabbles, he'd make the afternoon a time to play with either son, take them somewhere, go to one of their sporting events, or find something they were interested in and do it.

Much as work occupied his mind, he still wanted to stop at Mrs. Talucci's before he left. He had to organize care for Jeff during the day. Brian and his buddies had plans for the morning and afternoon and Paul wanted the house in some semblance of order when he returned. He enjoyed the vision of the boys downstairs waking up to Mrs. Talucci in charge. She'd have them scour every inch of house they'd come in contact with. Plus, if he could, he wanted to find out what had been bothering her. The fact that she wouldn't talk about what was wrong only accentuated his worries that it was serious. He hurried next door.

He walked into the kitchen, expecting from long familiarity to find Mrs. Talucci sipping espresso coffee and reading a book at the kitchen table. On a Saturday she'd have done the dishes and had bread baking in the oven for any weekend feasts her family had planned. But this time Paul found no warm smell of freshness from the oven and no Mrs. Talucci at the table.

The niece who met him at the door said that Mrs. Talucci was downstairs. Turner found her in the reconverted basement, one of the many projects he'd done for her in return for her watching Jeff and Brian. It had taken him six months but the result was excellent. He had eliminated any dampness and smell, paneled the walls with pine, and installed floor-to-ceiling bookcases to hold Mrs. Talucci's ever-expanding collection. The shelves overflowed with everything from weighty tomes to the most recent popular fiction. In the center of the room were the only two chairs. Both black leather with footstools in front of them, a glass-topped table between them, on top of which was a reading lamp with shaded bulbs reaching to both chairs.

Mrs. Talucci sat in the chair on the left. She wore a faded flower-print house dress and purple slippers. She glanced up at Paul and put her book aside. Paul noted the title: Tolkien's *The Lays of Beleriand*.

He saw tired eyes, listless hands, wisps of white hair not caught and pulled back into Mrs. Talucci's usually perfectly constructed bun at the back of her head. He seldom noticed her wrinkled face and the flesh drooping on her arms and elbows. Today she looked over a hundred.

Her "good morning" seemed beyond age and weariness.

Paul sat down in the other chair.

"What's wrong, Rose?" he asked.

She held his gaze with her dark brown eyes. "I have cancer," she said. Before he could respond, some of her old fire and command returned. "I do not want sympathy. I do not want pity. I'm ninety-two years old. I certainly did not expect to live forever. The hard part is that after telling the family, they're going to be over here invading my privacy, slobbering all over. I don't want tears and confessions. I've had a good life, but I'm old. That's what you do when you're old, die."

"Rose . . . "

"And don't you get all slobbery."

Paul felt the tears in his eyes.

"I'm not going to die today or tomorrow. Before the doctor could say it, I told her there wasn't much point in painful treatments at my age. The cancer's beyond the point of doing anything about, anyway." She ended much more wistfully, "I would prefer, however, not to die in pain."

"Rose . . . "

"But the doctor didn't know about that, or how long I'd live. The weasel wouldn't give me a straight answer. All she'd say is cancer moves slowly in old people." She snorted. "How lucky for us."

"I'll do anything I can to help," Paul said.

She smiled her old lively, affectionate smile, "Thank you. I hadn't wanted to tell you until all the final tests were done. I met with the doctor yesterday. You're the first one I've told." She closed her eyes and sighed. "At least I beat old Ethel Watson. She lived to be ninety-one, the old witch."

Rose was referring to an old rival who had lived a block over for eighty-five years. Their children had fought when they were little and Ethel had tried to get one of Rose's daughters sent to an orphanage around 1920. Rose had never forgiven her.

She stood up. "I've been expecting you. You'll need help with the boys this morning."

"It's not necessary. . . ."

"I am not about to physically collapse," she said. "I can do today what I did yesterday and my mind hasn't developed defects overnight. The kid who got murdered—I saw you on one of the twenty-four-hour Chicago news stations. You're on the case and you've got to go to work. Brian's got a herd of boys that need ordering. Jeff needs watching. Of course I'll do it."

Paul gave up any attempt at protest. Mrs. Talucci, sick or well, had an air of command it was useless to attempt to override. That she had gone to the doctor on her own and taken the news without family around was typical of the way she'd lived her life.

In the car on his way to work, Paul found himself unable to control his tears. Instead of driving straight to the station, he took Congress Parkway out to Grant Park, parked on Columbus Drive, put a quarter in the meter, and walked to the pedestrian crossing for Lake Shore Drive. He knew he'd be late for meeting Fenwick, but at the moment he didn't care.

He walked slowly along the lake shore. He realized he'd known Rose was old, but understanding she would die because she was old didn't make the reality of her eventual loss easier to accept. It was hard to imagine her not being there.

Rose Talucci was more precious to him than anyone except his sons. Paul's wife, Mary, had died when Jeff was born. In the months before his second son's birth, Paul had come to accept his own being gay. He'd come to love his wife as a friend and her death had pained him deeply. He sometimes wondered what would have happened had Mary lived and he'd come out to her. Certainly their marriage would have been over. It was one of the great "what if's" of his life.

Rose had become a large part of Paul's family. He loved her fiery spirit and joy in living, her jokes and laughter. She'd had to overcome a tough early life in a dirt-poor hovel in the Taylor Street neighborhood in the early part of the century. He would miss Rose and her fabulous dinners. He loved the late night snacks she'd throw together and insist he eat after he came home very late and she'd put the kids to bed. They'd talk for hours. She had insight and wisdom. He would miss building and fixing things for her. Mrs. Talucci was one of the few people he would trust implicitly in anything. He would miss that and all the rest.

He found himself at the foot of the Adler Planetarium. Already complements of school buses were disgorging school kids for visits here and at the Field Museum across the street. Even on Saturdays, hordes of kids descended on the place in vast multitudes. The shouting children's voices punctuated by adult commands brought him out of his reverie. He turned back toward the car.

Rose was still alive and would make the most of every moment, now and as she had throughout her life. When the time came, he'd do everything he could to ease any suffering. As he pulled up to the station, he realized he'd have to tell his own kids about Rose's illness. He closed his eyes and shook his head. Sometimes an enormous day's work ahead wasn't a bad thing.

He found Fenwick, the commander, and six uniformed cops on the fourth floor shoving desks aside, dragging cabinets hither and yon, plugging in phone jacks, and toting piles of paper. The fourth floor of the old complex was mostly storage space for musty police department records which they kept promising would some day be put on computers. They could wait until the turn of oblivion for such a happenstance.

Fenwick said, "We've got a 'task force.' The police in Kenitkamette and Chicago will be cooperating."

"And good morning to you," Turner said.

"You'll need to start sorting assignments," the commander told them. "Spend some time on that and then begin on the interviews out in the suburbs."

"We've got nothing in the city?" Fenwick asked.

"You tell me. You're still in charge. Do it."

Turner and Fenwick trooped down to their desks one floor below.

"We got trouble, right here in River City," Fenwick said.

"I'm the one who's supposed to quote show tunes," Turner said.

"You know, you never do."

"Maybe one of my gay genes is defective."

"I thought it was the anterior hypothalamus."

"You memorized that?"

"I read all the gay shit in the papers."

"And I'm eternally grateful and not interested at the moment. This case is going to be a pain in the ass. All calls connected to it are being directed to . . . ?"

"I've got somebody screening them already. The wackos have begun to report in."

In any high-profile case the absence of leads was seldom a problem. Every nut case in the city, from people who spotted UFOs to those who got the shakes and vapors waiting for the end of the world, would call in with their theories, sightings, facts, wayward thoughts, and tales of aliens. A few you might be able to discard, but almost every one of them had to be followed up. If you didn't, you risked the danger of missing the one call that was actually genuine and could give a real clue or maybe even break a case wide open.

"We have the people to cover the crazies?" Turner asked.

Fenwick hunted through a pile of papers on the left side of his desk. "For all the follow-ups for all calls from the public. Commander gave me a list of five people for today. We'll get more tomorrow." He found the list and handed it to Turner.

"We have to get organized," Turner said. He stood up and reached for the bulletin board on the right side of his desk. He took down the scattered notes and wanted posters and put up Fenwick's list on the now blank three- by five-foot cork. In an hour it was filled with lists of people and their assignments. Cops would return to the scenes of both crimes. Every employee of the parking garage would be questioned. The neighborhood around Lumber Street would be canvassed. The owners of the building would be found and talked to. Someone would speak again with the kid who found the body. Every playmate and friend of his who might have gone there that day or any other would be questioned. Every employee of any nearby McDonald's would be interrogated in case the wrappers in the building had anything to do with where the murderer might have been beforehand.

All these people would be asked about anything or anyone suspicious that they had seen or noted prior to or on the day of the crime. If the murderer had staked out the killing space, then he or she might have been noticed.

Every kid who knew the dead kids at school would have to be talked to. It was a tremendous task, but each interview had to be recorded on paper. Anything promising would be passed to Turner and Fenwick, and even then they'd have to find time to read over all the unpromising reports. They had to have a handle on every aspect of the case: something a uniformed officer might consider unimportant could turn out to be significant, but Turner and Fenwick would probably be the only ones to know that. So they'd read everything that came in.

They'd asked the Crime Lab to return to the abandoned factory at Lumber Street and go through every room on every floor for any more traces of what had happened.

It was noon before they left the station. They grabbed a sandwich at Fred's Deli, under the Metra train tracks on Harrison Street. They ate in the car as they drove north. As they crossed the border into Evanston, Fenwick asked, "What's wrong?"

"Huh?"

"You haven't said a word since we finished eating. You've been preoccupied all morning. I thought it was the case, but something's bugging you."

Turner told him about Rose Talucci.

Fenwick listened quietly. When Turner finished, he said, "I'm sorry, buddy. I know how close you and your kids are to her. If I can help, let me know."

"Thanks."

"You going to tell the kids?"

"Yeah. I don't know how."

"It's going to be tough. She's been the closest thing to a mother they've had."

"I know."

They let a companionable silence, borne of many years as partners, pass between them for the next few miles. Finally Turner said, "What do we have first?"

"List is in the notebook," Fenwick said.

Turner dug through the official papers and found the notes written on tiny graph paper. He and Fenwick had gotten into the habit of writing on graph paper and ordering all their notes not requiring an official form on the small squares. These often seemed an oasis of orderliness amid the violence and chaos that filled their days.

Turner read through the list. "The Kenitkamette School District people are cooperating in letting us use the high school."

"That Chief of Police, Robsart, said they'd been real helpful. Best place for it."

Turner nodded agreement.

"They also said they were going to have grief counselors ready for any kids who needed it," Fenwick said.

"They were well liked and popular?" Turner asked.

"That's what somebody said last night. I wish they weren't. It would be great if the first kid or teacher we talk to says he hated the both of them and he's the killer."

"I'd say you'd been listening to fairy tales, but I've barely said a word."

"You got the directions someplace?"

Turner pulled them out. Kenitkamette High School put all the other schools on the North Shore to shame. New Trier could brag, but Kenitkamette was the equal of any private high school in the country in facilities, scholarship, test scores, and alumni as graduates of Ivy League schools and heads of corporations.

The campus seemed more like a college's, with wide spaces between buildings, brick walkways among swards of green grass, and trees bountiful with October's harvest of red, gold, orange, and brown leaves. Today the winds were down and a hint of summer's warmth had returned to the air.

They met the Kenitkamette Police Department brass in the superintendent's office. Turner thought he'd entered the plush

45

palace of an ancient emperor. Lavish wall hangings, solid teak desk, genuine antique lamps and knickknacks, including a nineteenth-century Chinoiserie lacquer tea caddy. The carpet matched the hues of the autumn afternoon that Turner could see through an enormous picture window.

Chief Robsart said, "I've managed to get a huge number of people here, or coming in for interviews. Everybody wants to help. Lots of people think of the North Shore as clannish or snobbish, but these people knew and liked the Goldsteins and Douglases. Community groups, parents, kids—everybody's spread the word. We've had over three hundred volunteers for preinterviews. I'm afraid no one in this crowd is going to have anything bad to say about those boys. Maybe nobody thought negatively about them."

"It would be a first," Turner said.

"Somebody felt negative enough about them to kill them," Fenwick said.

"Well, you're not going to find that among the people we've had in here. I've got the people who knew them best set up to talk to you."

"Prior to last night, any problems with the families?" Fenwick asked. "Domestic calls?"

"I checked to be certain. None. These are good people."

"No way to confirm when they got where they got, and if they stayed there?" Fenwick asked.

Robsart shrugged. "I have no reason to doubt them."

They discussed logistics. The Kenitkamette cops would continue interrogating people and weed out the ones who knew very little or were just hangers-on. Anyone with something negative to say would be moved up to the top of the list of people for the Chicago cops to talk to. Until somebody with something rotten to say was found, Turner and Fenwick would interview the closest friends and teachers.

They asked the Kenitkamette cops about the presence of sex toys and mentioned the notebook filled with the Satanic alphabet.

None of them had heard the remotest thing out of the ordinary connected with these two boys.

"We can ask around and see if anybody knows anything about that on the force," Robsart said.

They thanked her for checking.

"You interviewing the families again?" Robsart asked.

"Tentative meet at six, I think," Fenwick said.

"I heard their lawyer's going to be there," Robsart said.

Both Chicago cops raised inquisitive eyebrows.

"This is the North Shore. They're good people, but they can afford expensive lawyers. Up here being a cop is too much like being social arbiter most of the time. Real crime. . . ." She shook her head. "I don't envy you guys. To be honest, I'm glad it's not me in charge of this one."

The first teenagers they talked to burbled with information confirming that both boys had been well liked and popular. They were kind to other kids in that aristocratic-athlete way that long-familiar popularity, good looks, natural athletic ability, and experience with girls gave to some boys at an early age. All expressed, as did everyone they questioned that day, astonishment about sexual toys or Satanism. All said they'd never heard either boy discuss or even hint about such things.

Jake Goldstein's girlfriend, Sally Baker, came in around two-thirty. She wore gray sweat pants and sweatshirt. She carried tissues in one hand. Her eyes and nose were red.

"We'd like you to try and help us find whoever killed Jake and Frank," Turner said.

"I don't know if I can help," she said in a wispy voice. She wiped her eyes with a tissue. "I'll do what I can."

"When did you meet Jake?"

"In freshman year, but we didn't start going out until this August. He dated another girl for a couple years, but she left for college this year and she dumped him this summer before she left."

"He feel bad about that?"

"He cried on my shoulder. We've been friends a few years, but I didn't get him on the rebound. Our love was genuine. He was the most attentive guy I ever dated. He brought me only the nicest little memory gifts of our first kiss, first date."

"Did he have any enemies at school?"

"None. Nobody was even jealous. He was always kind to everybody."

"Any gang activity he might have gotten involved in? Upset somebody?"

"No. That's impossible."

"He ever do drugs, have drugs?"

"No. He was really clean. He was an athlete and took pride in it."

"Alcohol?"

"No. He was always concerned about driving sober."

Fenwick asked, "Do you know if he always wore his underwear?"

"As far as I know. He always did when. . . ."

The cops sat quietly.

"You know, when we'd make out. I knew."

"We found several sex toys in his room," Fenwick said. He listed them.

She gaped at him.

"He ever show them to you?"

"I've never. . . . Jake? I don't believe it. He wasn't that kind of guy."

They let the ensuing silence build for half a minute, then Turner asked, "Anything unusual about him at all?"

"He was just an all-around good guy."

They let her go a few minutes later. "I'm going to get real tired of this real quick," Fenwick said. "Saints don't get murdered."

Douglas's girlfriend told about going with him for two years. Claimed never to have fought with him. She knew nothing about a possible interest in Satanism.

Bob Elliot was a teacher who had known both boys since freshman year. "I taught them English freshman year, and they came out for the school play last year. I drove them home once after play practice when Frank had forgotten to tell his parents they needed a ride."

"How'd the two of them get along?"

"I never heard of any fights between them. They'd laugh and make jokes in an easy way. Frank could tease a little too much at times, but Jake was always a good sport about it, if not an actual antidote to Frank's strange sense of humor."

"No fights ever?" Fenwick asked.

"No. Great kids. The kind you'd like to have for friends when they're adults."

Jake and Frank's best friend on the team was Bob Talbot. They talked to him about four o'clock. He was the size of a defensive lineman on a pro football team. He kept wiping tears on the sleeve of his letterman's jacket.

"They were both cool," Bob said. "Best friends a guy could want. We hung around together a lot."

"Any enemies?"

"Nobody. Even on the team. They were the leaders. Everybody looked up to them. Whether we won or lost, they led the line for congratulating the other players."

"How about Jake breaking up with his former girlfriend?"

"Caroline? She was nice enough, but she was on her way to college. Guess she didn't want some high school guy dangling around her neck."

"He wasn't mad?"

"He was real broken up. One night after a few beers he cried for hours."

"He drink often?"

"Hey, it was no big deal. Most of the guys have a beer or two at a party. Nobody got uptight about it."

"Any problems with gangs? Drugs? He turn somebody in?"

"Nah. Most real athletes don't have time for that drug stuff. Neither of those guys would touch anything illegal."

They asked about sex toys and Satanism.

Talbot simply looked confused. "They never talked about that kind of stuff. Guys brag about sex, but nobody talks about intimate stuff like that. That religion stuff doesn't sound like Frank."

"Anything you can tell us about either one, anything at all that seemed odd in the past few weeks, no matter how unimportant you think it is?"

The boy scratched his burr-cut head and finally said, "Frank and Jake were the two straightest arrows ever. I'll miss them." And he began to bawl.

At five, they talked to the coach of the football team. He continued the litany of sainthood that everyone else had repeated. Kept their grades up. No problem in class. No problem on the field.

At six, Turner and Fenwick looked through the files the school district kept on the boys. Each folder bulged with registration forms, standardized test scores, medical reports, IQ scores, and notes from teachers. They were both B students with IQs in the lower 120s. The cops found nothing but glowing praise about the two boys' characters. Immediately after finishing with that paperwork, they met with the cops who had been conducting the other interviews.

Half an hour later Fenwick said, "They were saints."

Everybody nodded heads. Fenwick exhaled a gargantuan sigh. "Get the paperwork to us as soon as you can." He and Turner left to talk to the families.

In the car, Fenwick said, "I am depressed."

"We get everybody's movements for Thursday night?"

Fenwick pointed to a box in the back seat. "Somebody handed that to me as we left."

A Kenitkamette cop had asked each interviewee about their whereabouts on Thursday night. They tried to make it a routine and simple thing so that no one would take umbrage. The teenagers had been generally cooperative, a few of the adults hostile, but all had complied. Turner reached back and picked up the box. Each piece of paper had a person's name, address, and probable whereabouts, for that night.

Turner riffled through them. "We've probably got a couple hundred here."

"I dare you to rip them into a thousand pieces and throw them out the window."

Turner tossed them into the back seat. "Later."

"We should interview that former girlfriend of Goldstein's."

"Yeah. You know, I wonder if the Douglas kid still had his underwear on?"

"The killer says, 'Excuse me, would you take off your pants, give me your underwear, put your pants back on, and by the way, pow, you're dead'?"

"I am not in the mood for kinky on this."

"I'll let the killer know."

F O U R

A block away from the Goldstein home a clutch of reporters were gathered around several squad cars. The local cops had the street blocked off. Turner and Fenwick showed their identification to the cops on duty. One of the reporters began drifting over and the others followed. Fenwick sped off before they could overrun the car.

At the house they found the Goldsteins in the same room as the day before. A woman in a red wool suit shook hands with them. She was introduced as the family lawyer, Jennifer Edwards.

After they were seated, Turner said, "I'm afraid we haven't been able to find out much today." He gave them an outline of what they'd done.

"There must be something," Mrs. Goldstein said when he was finished.

Edwards said, "I've talked with Chief Robsart in Kenitkamette, and after listening to her and what these two officers have said, I'm of the opinion that everything is being done that can be done. The police are trying their best."

Turner didn't know if he appreciated or was annoyed by the vote of confidence.

Edwards continued. "You need to ask my clients questions that may be painful to them. I've let them know what is standard procedure in this type of case. As they said last night, they wish to cooperate any way they can. You already know that they were at a dinner in Kenosha until late?"

Turner nodded.

"How else can we help?" Edwards asked.

"Who knew the boys were going to the game?" Turner asked.

"It wasn't a secret," Ken Goldstein said. "I suppose their friends. I was given the sky box tickets for all the home games by alumni of St. Basil's University. None of them would know whether or not I'd be at a specific game. I often gave the tickets away. I let my son use them once before. That time he took his girlfriend."

"Who knew they were going to stop by and talk to the team members afterwards?"

"The same people who knew they were going to the game, I'm sure. The boys had been talking about the game for quite some time."

At that moment the Douglases arrived. While Edwards was not their lawyer before the incident, she said that she had talked with them and would be acting in that capacity for the moment.

Turner and Fenwick asked the same questions of the Douglases as they had of the Goldsteins with the same results. No helpful information.

"All day today we got extremely positive comments about both your boys," Fenwick said. "They were well liked by everyone, which doesn't help us pinpoint anyone who might want to do them harm. Is there anybody you can think of any time in their lives who didn't like them, had a bad experience with them?"

All four parents thought for a minute, but when they spoke it was with weary bafflement. None could remember anything the boys had done that could in any way be connected to murder.

After further fruitless probing Turner and Fenwick left, ran the gauntlet of the press, and drove off.

"Gonna be a mob of those back at the station," Fenwick said.

"Something to look forward to," Turner said.

"It's only nine. We got time to look for Goldstein's girlfriend?"

"She's at Northwestern, which is on our way back. She's living in a college dorm. I hope she's around. I doubt if it's too late to visit."

"Is it ever too late in a dorm to visit somebody, and when it's a murder case, do we care?"

Caroline Toomey lived in Ingles Hall on the Northwestern campus. Turner and Fenwick reported to the security office first and then proceeded to the dorm. It was between the drama and film building and the library.

A few students lounging in the lobby looked at them curiously as they asked for Caroline. The switchboard operator called up to her room. In a few minutes she bounced down the old wooden stairs. They sat in an alcove of a room that had wood-paneled walls and multicolored leather chairs.

Caroline turned out to have long, honey-colored hair and a slender figure. Her skin was flawless, with only the merest traces of makeup to emphasize the perfection. She greeted them with a cheerleader's smile and enthusiasm. She wore a T-shirt that clung to what even Turner recognized was a figure that Fenwick would refer to as a "header."

Caroline said, "I heard about Jake. It was awful."

"We're hoping you can tell us something that would help us catch the killer," Fenwick said.

"I'll do what I can," she said. She tucked her feet up under her and gazed at the detectives evenly.

"When was the last time you saw him?" Fenwick asked.

"Months ago, at a party. We talked a little. He seemed friendly. I met his new girlfriend."

"Why did you break up?" Fenwick asked.

"Jake was really sweet, but he was such a kid, really. He cared about sports so much. I enjoyed them, but not like he did. Plus I was going away to college. He was nice, but I'd started to meet a more serious crowd. I have my future to think about. He took it pretty well. I know some of my friends have to put up with some of that 'I-can't-live-without-you' crap, but Jake seemed to be okay. He felt bad, and so did I, but I knew it was over."

"Northwestern isn't that far away from Kenitkamette," Fenwick said. "I wouldn't call it 'going away' to college."

"It was such a different world. It might as well have been a thousand miles."

"He have any enemies that you know of, anybody with any kind of grudge at all?"

She thought a minute. "Well, me maybe, because of our break-up, but I don't think I was ever an enemy. I think he got over it. I mean, we talked and stuff after. If I hadn't gone to college, I think we'd have stayed friends."

"Anybody else?" Fenwick asked.

She drummed her nails on the leather armrest. "I know one gay guy came on to him at a party. Jake told me about it later. Said he turned him down. Don't know if the gay kid was upset or not."

"You know his name?"

"Ed Simmons. He's still a senior there."

"Did getting propositioned upset Jake?"

"I'm not sure. He was always so polite to everybody, but he acted a little odd about it, like maybe it did bother him but he didn't want to talk about it. I know gay and straight guys here and it's no big deal about who asks who out. Jake was just a little inexperienced, I think."

"How well did you know Frank Douglas?"

"Barely at all. He was sort of creepy."

"How so?"

"I think he was into Satanism-type stuff. He wore some symbol pinned to his leather jacket. He said it was for a rock band, but I thought it was some Satanic thing. I mentioned it to Jake once, but he laughed and said Frank liked to shake up other kids."

She said she never saw Jake wear any Satanic symbols or do anything but poke fun at Satanism in a mild way. She also didn't know any of Frank's friends who might know more about his connection to Satanism.

"When we found Jake, he didn't have his underwear on."

Caroline laughed.

Both detectives raised quizzical eyebrows.

"I shouldn't tell you this," she said, "it's a little embarrassing, but well. . . ."

"Go ahead," Fenwick said.

"When we went out on dates or when Jake thought it was a big occasion, he wouldn't wear his underwear. He told me he wanted to feel completely unencumbered." She laughed again. "He had a thing with wearing dress pants so that no lines showed. His pants would hang without the slightest wrinkle from his hips to his shoe tops. I think he thought it was studly. For a while I did too. Seeing him in his tux at the junior prom last year and knowing he didn't have his shorts on was a little bit of a turn-on then. Now I think it was just part of his getting used to being a man. Men are funny about stuff like that, but I think he wore his underwear most of the time. I don't think he wanted to undress in the locker room and have the guys see he didn't wear any. Guys are funny."

"He do anything else unusual that was kind of personal that might have bothered him?" Fenwick asked. "We found several dildos and some leather clothing among his stuff."

"Like a leather jockstrap and a studded belt?"

The detectives nodded.

"Well," she said, and looked at them from lowered eyelids, "I don't know how unusual this was, but he. . . ." This time her hesitation lasted more than a minute.

The cops waited as they'd been trained to do. Waiting for someone to talk and trip themselves up was second nature after this many years as detectives.

"He . . . I'm not sure how important this is." She looked at them but they waited for her.

"Well, he . . . when we'd start to make love, he couldn't last very long. Most of the time . . . he'd, you know, a few seconds after we'd be naked, he'd be done."

"Did this bother him?" Fenwick asked.

"I think it did. I tried to be nice about it. One of his friends on the team gave him the leather stuff. Said it might make any sex he had more enjoyable. I managed not to burst out laughing. I refused to use any dildo. It was gross. Jake put on the leather stuff once, and it seemed to make him a little more confident, but the next time, well, the old problem came back. I told him the kinky stuff wasn't one of the reasons we were breaking up, but it was. I just didn't want to hurt his feelings. Boys are so fragile."

"Where were you Thursday night?" Fenwick asked.

"Play practice until late and then talking with friends until about two."

She gave them the name of the kid who gave Jake the sexual materials. Other than the personal peccadillos, she knew nothing helpful.

In the car Turner said, "I don't know if I'd be happy or not, being dropped by somebody like that."

"Nobody that beautiful ever gave me more than one look," Fenwick said. "They'd never date me. Hell, if I dated somebody as beautiful as she is, I'd probably blow my wad after a few seconds, even at my age."

"You've got Madge. She looks great."

"She's nearsighted and refuses to wear her glasses unless she's driving. Did that even when she was a kid. I made sure I drove everywhere while we dated. She never got a good look at me before we got married."

"What did she do when she did get her first good look at you?"

"It was too late by then. We were in love."

"Kid wore his underwear for his new girlfriend," Turner said, "and didn't show her any sex toys."

"Maybe Caroline's rejection made him shy."

Turner leafed through his notebook for the list of kids who had been interviewed. "The guy Caroline Toomey mentioned as our porno peddler isn't here," he said.

"We'll have to talk to him. Probably means another trip back here tomorrow, but I don't have the remotest faith that these people up here will give us the slightest clue."

They got back to the station five minutes after midnight. Since they had left this morning the number of newspeople had expanded. Even at this late hour they clustered around Turner and Fenwick's car. The questions were pointed and the persistence with which they were asked almost irrational. Cameras and microphones were poked and shoved in their faces. This was not a good way to get a quote out of Fenwick.

He bellowed angrily when one of the cameras banged into his side. The crowd stepped back when his animal roar split the night. The cops took the opportunity to rush into the station.

The commander met them on the fourth floor. "Anything?" he asked.

"Nothing," Turner said.

They told him what they'd done that day.

"You've got half a million more reports to go through." The commander indicated the stacks piled on the tables next to the corkboard, which filled an entire wall on the fourth floor.

A third of the corkboard was filled with still photographs from the scenes of both crimes—the dead bodies from every possible angle, shots of the entire room in the first case and the surrounding garage in the second. The pictures were silent sentinels of death hanging over everyone who worked on the fourth floor.

Turner and Fenwick had seen thousands of death scene photographs. They would go over them shot by shot later. For now they glared at the mounds of work below the pictures.

"I had them do some sorting as they put the stuff up here.

Evidence reports and Crime Lab examinations start on the right. I've got you lined up to talk to the Bears players the boys spoke with after the game. You'll be going to tomorrow morning's practice. Uniforms have canvassed a three-block radius from the scene. Not many people around. They got admitted to the surrounding buildings. Most are abandoned and in about the same shape as the one the murder happened in. Didn't find anything."

After the commander left, Turner and Fenwick found two chairs with rollers and began at the left of the tables. They pored over reports and commented to each other if they found something significant.

When Fenwick got to the medical examiner's report, he pointed to the third page. "Killer used a .38 automatic," Fenwick said. "Definite confirmation that Goldstein got shot up the ass twice." He handed a copy of the report to Turner.

"That's why the angle of those abdomen wounds seemed funny to me," Turner said. "He was shot up and in, and they came out from the body." He glanced down the form. "Shot six times total, once in the head."

"Why shoot him twice up the butt? The killer missed the first time?"

"Or he enjoyed the effect and said twice is better?"

"Anything besides the marks on his wrists and ankles that showed that Goldstein fought back at all?" Fenwick asked.

"No traces of foreign matter under the fingernails. Goldstein didn't scratch the killer," Turner said.

"Rope killer used to tie him was gone," Fenwick said. "Killer must have taken it with. Funny. He couldn't get more rope?"

"Maybe he wanted to clean up after himself," Turner said.

"I like an anal-retentive murderer," Fenwick said.

"Not amusing," Turner said. "In fact, kinda gross, if not totally disgusting."

"Yeah, well, cheap cop gallows humor ain't easy."

They worked in silence for several minutes until Fenwick said, "You'd think a kid like that would fight back."

"We do have abrasions on wrists and ankles."

"But wouldn't he fight when the guy was tying him up?"

"No way to tell when he fought if he did. The room was mostly a mess with his blood, but I don't see anything that showed a fight happened. We were there. You care to venture an opinion that a fight took place?"

"No. Furniture didn't get tipped over because there wasn't any to move around or bust up. So, no proof of a fight. Killer held a gun on him all the time?" Fenwick turned a page on the report. "He was tied hand and foot, but you'd think he'd make some protest."

"Maybe he did. He could have broken the killer's arm in seven places for all we know."

"Doesn't say Goldstein was unconscious. He knew what was going to happen?"

"Can't imagine knowing I might be dead in seconds," Turner said. "Maybe one of the first shots had the kid in pain and agony and bleeding something awful." Turner shook his head. He flipped several more pages. "Listen to this. No drugs in either kid's system."

"Isn't the cliché if kids die, it's got to be drugs?"

"If it is, it isn't so in this case."

Fenwick sighed. "Are we agreed on the timing of this?"

"You've got to figure the Douglas kid died first. Otherwise you wind up having to control two athletic kids at the same time, and you have to drag both boys around town."

"So, the killer walks up to the two kids in the parking garage," Fenwick said. "He shoots one for whatever reason and makes the other go with him."

"And the threat he uses on Goldstein is that if you don't come quietly, you'll get what your friend got?" Turner asked.

"Makes reasonable sense."

"That how he got the kid to walk up all those stairs and down those halls in that abandoned factory?"

"Can't imagine that much carrying of a live, muscular teenager who's at least squirming."

"Maybe we've got a very muscular killer?"

They perused the reports in silence for a few moments. "Look at this," Turner said. Fenwick rolled his chair over. They gazed at the sheet of paper together. "Goldstein's balls were crushed with the ever-faithful blunt instrument," Turner said.

"I knew this was going to turn out to be kinky," Fenwick said. "I don't like kinky with my murders. I hate kinky."

"Where's the report on the other kid?"

They hunted it up and read. "No crushed balls or anything unusual," Fenwick said. "Just one shot to the head. Killed him instantly. Good. No kinky."

"Why'd he take the time to crush the kid's nuts?"

"Let's be sure to ask when we catch this creep. Goldstein's murder sure seemed like it had some kind of sexual connection. We got any cum traces?"

They hunted through the documents.

"Nope," Turner said.

"If not sexual, at least kinky," Fenwick said. "Of course, how can you have kinky without cum? If it's kinky, it's got to have cum."

"I always prefer cum with my kinky," Turner said.

"Just like you. Are we sure they checked? Where's the fluid report?"

"Here," Turner said. They looked at the lines of print. "Only one type of blood each place and no other fluids."

"Gotta be spit, sweat," Fenwick grumbled as he reread the section. He slowly flipped through several pages, then said, "Hey, check this out. Frank Douglas had a one-inch by one-inch tattoo of an upside-down pentagram on his left shoulder."

"Kid had to be more than dabbling or simply interested in Satanism if he went far enough to get a tattoo. Wonder if the parents knew? Maybe they were lying to us when we asked about Frank being into Satanism."

"Don't know about that," Fenwick said, "but would you know if Brian had a tattoo?"

"We went swimming on vacation last year. He doesn't have

61

one, unless it's on his butt or between his thighs, and if it is, I'm not sure I want to know about it."

Fenwick shook his head. "Kids getting tattoos."

"Too kinky for you?"

"That is not kinky, it's just dumb."

They perused reports for three hours. No one else was left on the floor when they decided to call it quits.

"What's everybody working on tomorrow?" Fenwick asked.

"We've got the Bears practice," Turner said. "I'm looking forward to that. We should try to arrive when they're changing clothes."

"I'm not going to be a part of some erotic crap. That's all I need is you running around with a hard-on."

"I won't be running around with a hard-on. I'll just be discreetly peeking at any sexy males. Like I've never had to hold you down when a sexy female wanders into your scope of vision."

"Not this week you haven't. I didn't figure you for the beefy-football-player type."

"I'm not, but maybe a quarterback or a kicker, or maybe a stray pass receiver might wander into view. At least I'll get a chance to look at them up close. You're jealous because it's not a women's locker room."

"I'm too tired to be jealous of anything or to even work up a letch for a naked nymphomaniac. What's everybody else working on tomorrow?"

Turner checked the charts. "Half the damn task force is tracking down leads from people that have called in."

"No doubt one is the killer trying in his or her own obscure way to confess."

"We've got reports to write and more reports from others to read. We better get some computer people up here collating data. We want to be able to organize things. I'll talk to the Watch Commander on our way out. He can try and get Blessing and his crew on it first thing in the morning."

Several years ago the Chicago Police Department had sent three cops to FBI headquarters to be trained in using a Rapid Start team. Since then, the department had set up its own Rapid Start team. This consisted of computer specialists who could be deployed within an hour to any area or district in the city. They would have laptop and desktop computers, telephone modems, and customized off-the-shelf computer software. They would take all the data collected by the task force and enter it into the computers, categorizing and organizing it at the same time.

They would also have access to over one thousand databases and four FBI mainframe computers at regional information centers. These could provide possible follow-up information, especially any cross-referencing of suspect profiles.

The watch commander grumbled about the lateness of the hour for such a request, but he promised to move on it as quickly as he could. Turner dragged himself to his car and drove home. He found the house quiet and both boys asleep. He dozed off to the comforting thought that they were trustingly in bed and at rest.

Paul awoke the next morning to a buzzing in his ear and pounding on his door. He heard Brian's voice, "Dad, you up? Your alarm's on. You've got a phone call."

It had been years since the wake-up music on his clock radio hadn't been enough to rouse Paul. Today he'd even slept through the annoying buzz of the alarm. He and Mary had gotten the alarm for a wedding present from his in-laws. He never knew if it was a subtle hint that they thought their daughter was marrying a lazy bum, or a simple but odd wedding present.

"Dad?" Brian called again.

"I'm up," Paul responded. He swung his legs out of bed.

"You've got a phone call," Brian repeated.

Paul threw on some jeans and padded downstairs. He picked up the kitchen extension. Jeff was at his place poring over a book by

Walter R. Brooks. Brian was at the counter chopping vegetables. Paul thought he would puke if he had to eat one of his older son's omelets crammed with broccoli and carrots.

The commander was on the other end. "I've just gotten a call from the mayor himself. He was actually very reasonable, but he wants a press conference explaining what we're doing. He wants us to be aware of public relations. He wants us to plead for help from every citizen."

"We don't need more calls from the people. We need less."

"I know, but the mayor asked. So we're going to do it in an hour. You need to get down here."

Paul sighed. He hurried his morning shower and managed to get away with eating several pieces of toast and downing a couple glasses of orange juice.

"What's wrong with Mrs. Talucci?" Jeff asked as Paul hugged his younger son on his way out the door.

Paul stopped. "What do you mean?" he asked.

"She seemed kind of tired yesterday. I did my homework, but she didn't check it over. She always does."

"Did Brian check it?"

"Yeah, but he's not as good at math as Mrs. Talucci."

"I'm not sure what's wrong," Paul said. "You have to hurry or you'll be late to church."

Paul wished the reminder about Mrs. Talucci's health hadn't been so direct this morning. He also hated being less than honest with either of his sons.

He tried calling Ben Vargas at home and on the private line at the service station. He got answering machines at both locations. Risking being late for the press conference, he drove the block and a half to the station.

No customers were using the gas pumps out front when he drove up. In back he found Myra Johnson pushing a disabled Porsche into a service bay. He lent her a hand. Myra had an incredible reputation among the expensive-foreign-car set in the city. They begged her to work on their cars. She prized her private time so she often turned them down. They even offered her enormous sums of money, but she worked for only a select number of people. Her being here on Sunday morning meant this was an especially prized customer with tons of money to pay for off-hour repairs.

After the car was inside, Myra said, "Ben misses you."

"Is he here?"

"Not yet. He offered to pick up some parts for me early today up on the North Shore. Friend of mine with a specialty shop agreed to open for me." She patted the hood of the car. "Bunch of people gonna make a ton of money on this little baby today."

Paul felt let down at Ben's not being around. "I love him," he said. "I miss him too."

"You've got choices to make," she said. Myra was also known for her bluntness. She very much approved of Ben and Paul's relationship and had urged them to move in together but both men claimed they weren't ready for that.

"We're working on the Goldstein murder," Paul said. "It's a tough case."

"They're all tough cases," she said. "How often do you meet a man who loves you? How often do you find somebody who likes your kids too?"

Paul didn't have time to argue, but he said, "I've got to make a living."

"You don't have to be a cop."

"It's what I do."

"Your relationship with Ben's your business," Myra said. "All I know is, Ben loves you. The more he doesn't see you, the more grumpy he gets around here." She smiled. "If nothing else, the man needs to get laid. When he doesn't get any, he's impossible to work for. Can't you give me a bit of a break?"

Paul was glad she'd lightened up some. Maybe she could tell how bad he felt. "Tell him I was here," he said.

"Send him some flowers or something," she said, then patted him on the shoulder. "I'll tell him you stopped by."

The autumn weather continued its turn for the pleasant. The wind came gently out of the south. Turner arrived at the station to find a seething Fenwick pulling his way through rows of folding chairs and the people in them in the squad room on the first floor. Fenwick saw Turner and hurried over.

"Press conference hasn't started," Turner said. "Tell me it's not because I'm late."

"It's not because you're late. Feel better?"

"A bunch. What's going on?"

"Commander decided to wait for more reporters. Some of the national news and the cable stations want live coverage. We've got television shit up to our necks here and I am pissed."

"Try not to rip any of their heads off, but my guess is you won't get a chance. I bet the Commander is going to answer most of the questions."

Some of the regular Chicago reporters had spotted them. A few began to drift over to talk to them. Turner told them they'd have to wait for the press conference. A couple of them began to get insistent, but the commander appeared at the podium and beckoned Turner and Fenwick forward. Television lights flicked on. Reporters settled down.

Turner and Fenwick stood on either side of the commander. Along with the two detectives, a lot of the police brass and representatives of the mayor's office clustered behind the podium.

A woman in a gray skirt and white blouse with a Peter Pan collar buttoned to the top asked the first question. She began with, "Commander Poindexter, do the police have any suspects at this time?"

They heard the litany of usual questions. "Do you have any leads? What are the police doing? Should the public be alarmed? What are you doing next?" And the confirm-the-rumors questions. "I heard they were into drugs, prostitution, throwing track meets and tennis matches."

The commander urged those who had any evidence of these charges to give it to the police. Turner knew they never would. They'd hide behind the inability to reveal their sources and never admit that these were questions dreamed up late the night before during the poker game at the most expensive hotel they could get their news organizations to spring for. Then the questions turned to the "Why don't you have suspects, leads, or an arrest yet?" variety. Some idiot from a national newsmagazine asked, "Why won't you give us a detailed rundown of exactly what the police have been doing? The public has the right to know."

Turner heard Fenwick growling deep in his throat. The commander abruptly ended the press conference.

They adjourned to the third floor. On top of his desk Turner found a message to call Ian Hume. A second form contained the name of the contact person at the Bears' training camp. He tried Ian's number at home and at the newspaper, but found him at neither place.

Up on the fourth floor the activity was impressive. Besides the regular task force people answering phones, writing reports, and chatting with each other, the Rapid Start team had deployed themselves in a section of the room near the floor-to-ceiling corkboard.

The watch commander of the twelve-to-eight shift had come through beautifully. The Rapid Start team, Jack Blessing and his crew, had been called in early that morning, long before the press conference started.

Jack Blessing was an African-American cop in his late twenties. Turner and Fenwick had worked with him before. He'd been among the first cops trained in the Rapid Start program. He was issuing brisk commands when he saw Turner and Fenwick and said, "We're ready here. Anything specific I can set up for you?"

For twenty minutes they discussed what they wanted from the computer. Blessing was so competent that Turner and Fenwick left most of the directing in his hands. If there was a way to solve the murder with a computer, Blessing would find it. They'd start by inputting everything about the dead boys: height, weight, color of eyes, names of friends, any scintilla of data that might relate to these kids would be on the computer. They knew Blessing would be one of the few cops who would put in as much time as they on the case.

They drove to the northern suburbs again, this time to the

Bears' training camp. Their contact turned out to be a guy in his early thirties who walked with a cane and spoke with an Eastern European accent. He'd played on the Bears' practice squad for seven years until an unfortunate tackle on a blown play ended his career and left him permanently deformed. He introduced himself as Malcolm Parushka. The few teeth that showed in his mouth were yellow and black, the diseased teeth of a man who hadn't heard the word "dentist" soon enough. He was pleasant and courteous to the cops in a very gentle, Old World way.

"I've mentioned to the players who talked to the boys that you would be here today. They are most eager to help. The young men made a very favorable impression on the people they talked to. I'll be happy to do anything I can, and so will anyone in the Bears' organization. It's just awful what happened to those boys."

"Were you the contact from the team who helped the boys that night?" Turner asked.

"Yes," Malcolm said. "They were amazingly polite and very excited. We try to be helpful to kids who are athletically gifted. Of course, it was very significant that they were connected to Ken Goldstein. To be honest, the boys wouldn't have been able to get in without that kind of connection. We can't have the players bothered by just anybody."

While they talked, he led them past a series of classrooms to a lounge paneled with pine. The chairs were all comfortable recliners. The room had a view onto the playing fields where they could see practice taking place in the distance. Malcolm excused himself to go get the team members.

"I'm not going to see naked football players," Turner said.

"Some days are like that," Fenwick said.

"Maybe at least they'll be all sweaty?"

"You could ask one for a date."

"I could flap my arms and fly to the moon too. At least I'll have been closer than any gay man I know to a real Bears player. I'll be able to look up front and close at sweat-stained practice clothes."

"Try not to leap out of your chair and molest too many of them. I'd like to get you out of here in less than five pieces."

They heard the clicking of cleats from the corridor. Moments later Malcolm and four players trooped in. They were Damien Durward and Larry Mannering, starting offensive linemen; Donald Waverly, special teams player; and Bill Marmion, acquired over the summer from the Canadian Football League as third-string quarterback. He had yet to take a snap this year in a real game. They mostly wore T-shirts and baggy shorts.

The comments flowed: "Great kids, really polite, not obnoxious like lots of teenagers." Fenwick strode to the window and turned his back on the players and the room as they prattled on in their praise. Turner sat up abruptly when one added to the litany: "I was supposed to meet them after I got done dressing." Fenwick returned to his chair.

Donald Waverly had made the remark. "They wanted to know what the swinging life of a bachelor football player was like. We were going to go to one of the places on Ontario Street and grab a bite to eat." Ontario Street in Chicago was rapidly turning into the place to be for all the young, trendier, with-it crowd.

Waverly looked to be younger than the other three players. Turner didn't remember his name from any newscast or newspaper report. His oversized sweatshirt was grass-stained and dirt-smeared. He wore black spandex under his practice shorts. Turner deplored this habit among sports team members. While jockstraps didn't allow for a lot of conjecture about crotch content, the baggy-shorts-over-spandex craze ruined tons of obscene speculation. Spandex and no baggy shorts would have been great, and perhaps naked and sitting in his lap best of all. He shook his head to clear the obscene speculations.

"Wasn't it kind of late to be going out?" Fenwick asked.

"It was a special night for them," Waverly said. "I'm not a big star. It's fun to sparkle for the peons."

"What happened?" Fenwick asked.

"They were supposed to drive back to the stadium with their car. They never showed up."

"What'd you do?"

"I was puzzled, but what could I do? I figured something happened, but I had no idea what. I went home and forgot about it until the next day when I heard about it on the radio."

"What time did they leave the locker room?" Fenwick asked.

"Must have been a little before eleven," Waverly said. "Most of the guys were gone when the boys walked out."

None of them saw the two boys after that, and none of them had anything else to add. The visit with Goldstein and Douglas had been a pleasant meeting with some nice kids. The cops left.

"So was it as exciting as you thought it would be?" Fenwick asked.

"What?"

"Being that close to the players?"

"Didn't even get a good whiff of sweat," Turner said.

"And you're dating Ben, so I didn't slip them secret mash notes with your signature on them."

"I appreciate that. I wouldn't mind another look at that Waverly guy. I wonder how he keeps that hair so perfect after sweating at practice. Hips that narrow and shoulders that broad should be illegal." Turner thought a moment. "I'm going to run his name through the computer when we get back. He's the only one so far who might have had some kind of contact with them at the critical time."

"Might as well," Fenwick agreed.

"I've got the address of the gay kid and the kink freak. We can get that out of the way while we're up here. We've got to get more on this Douglas kid and his tattoo, if we can."

They found the street listed in Kenitkamette for the gay kid and drove up to the house. It was two stories of rough-hewn stone sitting on an acre of forested land. A teenage boy with carefully coiffed long black hair answered the door. They identified themselves. He admitted he was Ed Simmons. He let them in.

"My parents aren't home," he said.

"We wanted to talk to you," Turner said. "About Jake Goldstein and Frank Douglas."

He led them to a library with floor-to-ceiling bookcases, filled not surprisingly with books. They sat on deep plush armchairs. Simmons had a slight figure. His skin was beautifully tan and absolutely smooth with no trace of beard. Turner doubted if he shaved once a month.

The boy sat completely still in his chair. His hands rested palm down on each armrest. His feet stayed flat on the floor.

"I don't see how I can help," Simmons said.

"We understand you had a problem with Jake Goldstein," Turner said. "We'd like you to tell us about it."

The eyes barely blinked as Simmons's head turned the minimum amount of space it took to look from one detective to the other.

"I . . ." The kid stopped.

"Did you come on to him one day?" Fenwick asked. "He turn you down? That upset you?"

"I'm gay, as someone has obviously told you, but I don't hide that fact. Gay teens can ask guys for dates just like guys can ask girls or girls can ask guys."

"Do most gay guys go after the high school big man on campus?" Turner asked.

"Sure they do. Why not? Anybody could be gay. He was always nice and polite to me. We were friends."

"Did he consider the two of you friends?" Fenwick asked.

"Sure. We had honors classes together. We'd done projects with each other since fifth grade."

"When'd you come on to him?" Fenwick asked.

"Last year. I'd had a lot to drink at a party. He knew I was gay. I figured if I didn't ask, I'd never know, and sometimes if the other guy's a little high, he might . . . fool around."

Neither cop said, "But he was dating girls." Turner's life had taught them that this was not necessarily a bright or helpful comment.

"What'd he say?"

"He looked at me a little funny and said, in that polite way he had, 'No thanks.'"

"His attitude toward you change after that?"

"I don't think so. We did our end-of-junior-year physics project together. We spent a lot of time with each other on it. We never talked about the night of the party."

"You didn't maybe try a little grab-ass? Pissed him off. You got embarrassed? Mad?"

"No, why should I? He said no and I respected it. I had no reason to kill him. Besides, I only asked Jake. I never asked Frank. He wasn't my type. I rarely ever even talked to Frank, and he was murdered, too. Why would I kill him? Besides, I was here. Home all last night."

"How well did you know Frank?"

"We weren't friends. We weren't enemies. He was just a guy around."

"He had a tattoo of an upside-down pentagram on his left shoulder."

Simmons frowned. He said, "That's kind of strange."

"Why?"

"There's a couple kids around into Satanism. I never pictured Frank as one of them. I figured he's too into sports and athletics. I guess you never know."

"How do you know it's a Satanic symbol?"

"They made all the kids watch this film when we were freshmen. It was about the evils of drugs and gangs and stuff. It was funny and out of date, but part of it was on Satanism. What that symbol means would be fairly common knowledge among kids. At least those who were paying attention instead of falling asleep or making out during the movie."

"Who was into it at school?"

"I'm not sure. I know one kid got suspended last year for wearing a T-shirt with a Satanic symbol on it. His dad threatened to take the school board to court. I'm not sure what finally happened, but he might know something."

He gave them the name and they left.

In the car, Fenwick said, "Kid's awful good with rejection."

"Maybe a little too smooth. I don't know. I know I never would have asked another guy for a date in high school."

"So he's another dead end?" Fenwick asked.

Turner repeated the cop truism, "Everybody's a suspect."

The kid who'd given the sex toys to Goldstein lived in a heavily wooded subdivision. The house itself was ultramodern. The mother was home and wanted to stay while they questioned her son. Jim Nolan said, "Ma, I can talk to them. I haven't done anything wrong. I'll call you if I need you."

Nolan was six feet three, with a toothy smile and a loose, easy way of moving his body. He wore pressed khaki slacks, a starched white shirt, and loafers with no socks.

"How well did you know Jake Goldstein?" Turner asked.

"We were friends. I'm sorry he's dead."

"We understand you helped him out with some sex toys," Turner said.

Nolan's face turned red. "Hey, that's private business."

"Not in a murder investigation," Fenwick stated.

Turner said, "We're trying to track down anything about his life that might give any clue to the murder. Most teenagers don't keep a supply of dildos."

"Well. . . ." Nolan rubbed his hands on his pants legs. "Do I have to tell this?"

The cops nodded.

"Well . . . it's like. . . . There's this place on Howard Street in Chicago . . . where kids can go and buy . . . like condoms and stuff. . . . They don't ask questions . . . or ask for ID." He took a deep breath. "Jake and I went there a couple times. We'd talk about sex and stuff, like guys do, and everybody knows about this place and we went. We kidded about a lot of the stuff. He must have gone there on his own a couple times."

"He never bought leather items or dildos while you were there?"

"No."

"You never gave him any?"

"No."

"Never talked about sexual problems?"

"No. He wasn't a virgin or anything. He was a regular guy." After finding out Nolan had been home the night before, they left.

In the car, Fenwick said, "Add a stop on Howard Street to our itinerary. Where's this Satanic kid live?"

They stopped at the Kenitkamette Police Station to see if Robsart had anything new and to get the next kid's address. The Kenitkamette Police Station was one story all of red brick, with window frames painted white, a green lawn, and shiny clean police cars in front.

They filled in Robsart on what they'd gotten so far. Then she said, "I've got a little bit for you." She punched her intercom button and asked the secretary to send in Officer Cook.

Moments later a slender man with blond hair and broad shoulders walked into the room. He wore the Kenitkamette police uniform. Robsart said, "Hiram, tell them what you told me."

The officer said, "The local teens are kind of my specialty. I relate with them okay. I know a little bit about this Satanism stuff among them. The kid you want to talk to is Arnie Pantera."

"That's the name we got."

"Arnie is one strange kid. He's come to my attention a few times. He's the type who puts the cat in the microwave to see what happens."

"He really did that?" Fenwick asked.

Robsart nodded. "When he was nine. I remembered it after Hiram reminded me. That was a few years ago."

Hiram continued, "He's been to some counselors. Never did anything specifically illegal. You heard about the Satanism T-shirt?"

Turner and Fenwick nodded.

"His parents backed him on the issue. That's still in the courts. We've never arrested him, but he's got a few strange friends. He connected to the murder?"

They explained how his name had come up.

74

Robsart gave them the address and wished them luck.

The Pantera home was an old Queen Anne–style edifice. Fenwick said, "The more of these homes I'm in, the more depressed I get."

"Just think of the inhabitants as possible murder suspects."

"You're a comfort."

A maid answered and ushered them into the hall. Neither parent was home. Arnie appeared at the top of a grand staircase. He was the palest human being Turner had ever seen, and thin to the point of emaciation. He wore black jeans, a plain black T-shirt, black tennis shoes, and a thin silver chain around his neck.

Turner and Fenwick introduced themselves.

Arnie whispered, "Welcome."

"We'd like to talk about Frank Douglas," Fenwick said.

"Of course." More whisper. Turner wondered if he ever spoke at full voice. He led them up the stairs, down a hall, and into a windowless room. A black patchwork quilt lay across the bed. All the wooden furniture was painted black as were the walls. The carpeting was blood red. The entire ceiling was a mirror. More than twenty candles burned on a dresser in front of another mirror.

Turner wondered how the kid could live in such surroundings.

Arnie reached into a closet and pulled out a full-length cape. He swirled it around, and after it had draped itself over his shoulders, he clipped it at his throat. The interior of the garment was more blood red, the exterior more black.

Fenwick pointed to the ceiling above and whispered, "At least he shows up in the mirror. I wish I had a silver bullet."

Turner muttered back, "That's for werewolves. We need a sharpened stake."

"Don't we keep those in the car?"

"I haven't seen any lately."

As they were whispering, the teenager switched on a light over a chair, thrust out his cape-covered arms, sedately lowered himself onto a cushion, then carefully adjusted his cape so that it concealed everything but the bottom of his sneakers, painted black over white. They could only see his face from his lips up. "Yes, gentlemen."

"Frank Douglas had a tattoo on his left shoulder."

"Yes, I know."

"Oh."

"Yes. I helped him select it."

"Frank was into Satanism?"

"Frank was a friend who searched for answers."

"Did you have them for him?"

"I try to help my friends."

Not once had his voice risen above a barely audible murmur. Turner and Fenwick, still standing, unbidden to sit and unwilling to plunk themselves on the bed, tried more questions. The kid gave vague answers to their probing. He'd been home alone in his room the night of the murder. He admitted to no secret cabals or death rituals.

Not learning anything helpful, they left. Fenwick let out a huge breath in the car. "We've just met one of the ten weirdest kids on the planet."

"Wait until *your* kids are teenagers."

"Your kid isn't nuts."

"Ever had one of his broccoli-and-asparagus omelets? Kid eats another vegetable, I'm going to ram a carrot down his throat until he gags."

"Most parents would kill for a kid like yours. Come on, admit it. This kid was sicko."

"I admit it. Feel better?"

"I'm a tough cop, but I don't think I want to talk to that kid in that room again. He was creepy. Let's eat on the way back to the station. After we eat, we can get depressed among our own kind about getting nowhere on this case."

"We should stop at the porn shop first. It's on our way back."

"They're going to remember one kid?"

"We gotta ask."

Fenwick grumbled all the way to Howard Street. They found

the Garden of Earthly Delights at the corner of Clark and Howard Streets. The window had a mannequin of a male with a well-stuffed string bikini and a female with an equally well-stuffed bra and a bikini bottom even skimpier than the male's. They were lounging on a blanket and staring off into the street. Small red lettering at the bottom right-hand corner of the window gave the name of the store.

Inside, the carpet was black, the walls deep red, and the ceiling consisted of black panels alternating with mirrors. The room was long and narrow, with types of exotic underclothes on hooks on the left wall. Glass cases on the right were filled with dildos of all sizes and shapes, cock rings, leather straps, and other intimate delights. Immediately in front of them was a condom stand, beyond which were racks of clothes: one each of leather vests, then pants, and finally jackets of enough types and styles to outfit several motorcycle gangs.

A young couple, male and female, holding hands and murmuring softly, stood in front of a rack of skimpy briefs for men. Behind the counter stood a man in mirrored sunglasses, bare chest covered by a leather vest, and tight blue jeans clinging to a torso that might have been in good shape a few barrels of beer ago.

They showed him their identification.

"You the owner?" Turner asked.

The man behind the counter turned his mirrored sunglasses at them and nodded his head maybe a quarter of an inch.

Turner took out a picture of Jake Goldstein and showed it to the man. "We're wondering if you remember this person being in the store?"

The mirrored glasses looked down a quarter of an inch for half a second.

"No," the guy said.

"What's your name?" Fenwick asked.

"Gordon."

"Gordon, do you sell to underage kids?"

"No."

"Okay, Gordon, you got a permit and building inspection certificates?"

"I paid."

It's hard to glare into mirrored sunglasses, but Fenwick tried. After half a minute of silence, Turner said, "Let's go."

Back at Area Ten headquarters they piled their lunch of take-out deli sandwiches on top of Major Crime Worksheets, Daily Major Incident Logs, and Supplementary Reports—all waiting to be filled out. The tedious process of documenting everything they'd done that day and catching up on what they hadn't had time to fill out earlier could take as much time as all they'd done so far.

Randy Carruthers bounced in as Fenwick took his last bite of dill pickle. Randy had his butt aimed for the edge of Fenwick's desk, but the bulky older cop had a glare and an open fist ready to swat the young cop away. The annoying detective stood next to the desk. He bounced on his toes.

"This is great. We've got all this overtime because everybody's so caught up with your murders."

"I'm glad you're happy," Fenwick said.

"I've never seen so many reporters outside," Carruthers said. "If I were you, I'd take one into your confidence and leak positive stuff to the press. That way you'll have one friend for sure with them."

"When'd you become a press relations expert?" Fenwick asked.

"There's supposed to be openings coming up in the department press office. You can get a promotion and work with the public. You don't have to worry about dead bodies all the time."

"Commander approve your transfer yet?" Fenwick asked.

"I talked to him once. He didn't encourage me." Carruthers shook his head. "Nobody around here ever encourages me."

"You tried the latest yet, Randy?" Fenwick asked.

"What?" Randy asked, eager that someone was taking a slight bit of interest in him.

"I heard it's all the rage, Bungee jumping without a cord."

Carruthers smiled for a moment, then a frown began to cloud his round features. Before he could respond, Carruthers's partner, Rodriguez, marched into the squad room, saw Carruthers, gave a sigh audible through the entire room, came over and clamped his hand around his partner's upper arm. "We've got a dead homeless person, Randy. Just your type of crime. Let's go." They trudged off together.

Fenwick wadded up the paper from his lunch and sailed it into the trash basket five feet away. He rummaged on top of his desk. "We got preliminary reports here someplace?"

Turner picked up an inch-thick pile of computer printouts from the top of his desk and handed half of them to Fenwick.

"Blessing's too damn efficient for his own good," Fenwick opined.

Beat cops had already talked to a number of people connected with the case. The canvass of the neighborhood, abandoned and deserted as it might have seemed, would take quite a while. Owners of businesses and buildings anywhere nearby would have to be tracked down. Turner and Fenwick would have to do follow-ups on many of these.

Of the documents Fenwick was grumbling his way through,

Blessing had flagged those of the most important people for immediate interviews. If at all possible Turner and Fenwick would contact the most significant ones today.

"Look at this shit," Fenwick growled after ten minutes of scanning reports.

"What?"

Fenwick held one up. "I don't even have to read this one. I know what it'll say."

"Who is it?"

"This is from the fast-food franchise employee. I can hear it now. It'll be this kid with huge zits. He'll tell us he saw somebody come in covered up to his elbows in blood and gore and that the guy ordered a Big Mac, fries, and a soft drink. He leaves and the kid doesn't tell anybody. People come into this McDonald's all the time for their after-murder snack."

Commander Poindexter entered and asked for an update. They told him what they'd done so far that day.

"What's next?" Poindexter asked.

Fenwick sighed, "We talk to"—he glanced at the forms—"the owner of the building, fast-food employees, the kid who found the body."

"Parents are bringing him in," Poindexter said.

"Probably want to pamper their little tyke," Fenwick said. "And we've got the owner of a nearby business and. . . ."

"I've got the idea," Poindexter said. He sat his butt on the edge of Fenwick's desk. Randy Carruthers would have gotten a swat; Poindexter received a thin smile. "This whole thing is hell," he said quietly. "I know you guys are busting your rears, probably haven't slept more than a couple hours."

They nodded.

"Can't be helped. We've got famous kids dead. Public doesn't like athlete heroes who are good kids to get killed for no reason. I don't like that."

"I'm not real fond of it either," Fenwick said.

Poindexter sighed. "I know. We're pushing everybody as hard as possible. Whatever you need, it's yours."

"I could use a signed confession from somebody," Fenwick said.

Poindexter often found Fenwick amusing. Not today. "You got people to talk to, get back out there," the commander ordered.

Turner and Fenwick plodded out to the car. "Who first?" Fenwick asked.

"How about the owner of the building?"

"Who's he?"

"She. Arancha Bizerkowitz."

"There's an ethnic joke waiting to happen."

"Just think, if she married you, she'd be Arancha Bizerkowitz Fenwick."

"Lucky her, maybe I'll stick with Madge. Where to?"

"Lake Shore Drive just north of Oak Street."

At the exclusive address a block away from the Drake Hotel, they spoke with the doorman who then phoned the woman they needed to talk to. They took an oak-paneled elevator up to the eighth floor, then walked down the hall to a wide-open door. Arancha Bizerkowitz bustled up to them from inside, "Come in, come in, you wonderful boys." She smiled and patted their arms and marched beside them, all the while making little squeaking and chirping noises. Arancha Bizerkowitz must have been sixty years old. She wore red plastic frame glasses, a flower-print blouse tucked into jeans that would have been fashionably tight on someone forty years younger and twenty pounds lighter.

She waved them forward dramatically into a room furnished in basic plastic, all created in primary colors. A bright yellow couch with red cushions and orange chairs with fuschia cushions were set around a blue coffee table on which were brightly colored candlesticks from Cec LePage. The carpet was a checkerboard pattern of pink and green.

She offered them coffee, tea, cookies, sandwiches, beer, or hard liquor.

Fenwick said, "Ms. Bizerkowitz, we need to ask you about what happened at your warehouse."

"Oh, my, yes. It was awful. Can you imagine? Those poor, beautiful young boys. Such nice families. I watched every game the father won for a championship. All the hugging among those boys! I think it's wonderful that men can hug today. We have too many macho men afraid of touching." She put her fingers in front of her mouth and squeaked.

Turner wanted to say, "Just the facts ma'am."

Fenwick asked, "Did you kill Jacob Goldstein and Frank Douglas?"

One hand dropped to her lap; the other flew to her chest. She made inarticulate burbling noises for half a minute. When she finally got her breath, she gave them a cheery smile and said, "Don't you boys try and be amusing. I'm just shocked that such a thing could happen. Why just last week I was talking to my neighbor Floribunda. She had an operation last year and doesn't get around much any more, but she almost got mugged walking right outside our building. You just can't walk anywhere any more."

She offered them refreshments again. Turner declined but Fenwick told her yes, please.

"You hungry?" Turner asked as she left.

"Anything to get her out of the room and not listen to that voice."

"Reminds me of the less pleasant aspects of fingernails on slate."

"I don't recall any pleasant aspects of fingernails on slate."

They heard Arancha returning. Before she was halfway into the room, Fenwick stood up and used his don't-fuck-with-me tone. "Ms. Bizerkowitz, we've got a murder to solve. I want one- or two-word answers to my questions."

One of the cardinal rules of detective technique was that when you had a witness or suspect talking, you never shut them up. In this case, however, Turner had no quarrel with Fenwick's method.

Arancha began to speak, but Fenwick took a step closer to her. He towered over her.

"One or two words," Fenwick growled.

She gulped as she gazed up at his massive bulk. She placed the tray of goodies on the blue plastic coffee table.

Fenwick asked, "How long have you owned the warehouse?"

"Well, my husband bought it before he died. . . ."

"How long?" Fenwick asked again.

She folded her arms over her chest, glared at Fenwick, and said, "Two years."

"How often are you there?"

"Never."

Turner said, "Ms. Bizerkowitz, it would help if we could have as much of a history of the building as we can get. As current owner, anything you can tell us might make a difference in our investigation. We can get the official records from the county, but if you could tell us a bit, it might help catch the killers."

She smiled at Turner but looked warily at Fenwick. "We lived in fifteen different states in twenty years. My husband began selling computers for a number of different companies, before he moved into developing interactive programs. We did well and he started investing in real estate around the country. Before we moved to Chicago, we lived mostly on the West Coast." She listed all the cities. "My favorite was El Paso. They had the nicest people. Once you've seen all the pretty neighborhoods, you realize that setting is nice but really, it's the people you meet, the ones who become your friends. That's what really counts."

She drew a breath and Turner quickly asked, "When did you move to Chicago?"

"About a year and a half ago. My husband bought the building a few months before we moved to town. He thought it might be a good investment. He died before he could do anything with it. I've been trying to sell it, but I haven't had any luck."

"Who was the previous owner?"

"I have no idea."

"And you have Illinois Safe Serve as security?"

"I think that's it. They look after a bunch of old warehouses and factories. They have offices in this dingy low-slung affair way on the west side of the city. My Alfred, he was my husband, took me there once. It was filthy. Dirt on the floor that hadn't been cleaned in years. They made a very bad impression on me, but they were cheap."

"A little more expense might have prevented a murder," Fenwick said.

She gave him a mystified look, but before she could launch into another spiel, they left.

As they drove to the McDonald's at 18th and Halsted, Turner said, "She would have stopped talking some time this century."

"She would have been dead long before then. If we had a tape of a conversation with her, no jury would convict me."

At the McDonald's they found that the "kid" they were supposed to interview was the thirty-five-year-old assistant manager. He was Hispanic, slender, with soulful eyes and what in nineteenth-century Europe would have been known as a dueling scar on his right cheek running from his ear to the corner of his mouth.

After introductions, they sat at the front of the restaurant.

"What happened Friday morning?" Turner asked.

"Guy came in here about one, just before we close. Really excited. Breathing hard. Arms waving around. Demanded all kinds of stuff. The other employees had rung off their registers. I took care of him."

"Can you describe him for us?"

"I've thought a lot about it since those two uniformed officers stopped in. He was white, probably in his thirties, thin. Short, black hair, I think. No glasses. Dark clothes, but I don't remember if they were jeans or anything. When he left, he got in a truck. It wasn't new. It looked real beat-up."

"Did you get the license number, color of the truck?"

"No, after he started his engine, I forgot about him. I wanted to get out of here, and I had a lot to do to shut the place down for the night."

Back in the car, Fenwick asked, "Is that a description of our killer?"

"Eating a full meal after committing murder? Beats the hell out of me. We've had killers who've eaten parts of victims, so I suppose a little snack after torturing and killing a couple guys can't be completely ruled out in the life of a deranged murderer."

"It could happen."

"We'll add it to the computer data. Hard to run around the city looking for a thin thirty-year-old."

When Turner and Fenwick got back to Area Ten headquarters, they found the parents of the kid who'd discovered Goldstein's body in the warehouse. They were talking to Commander Poindexter on the first floor of the station.

After the introductions, the mother asked, "Is our boy going to be safe?"

They were a Hispanic couple in their middle thirties.

"We just want to talk to him, see if he can give us some memories. Maybe think of something important."

"We punished him for playing where he wasn't supposed to and for skipping school," the mother said. "Our boy, Herman, says that the kids in the neighborhood hung out there all the time, up to the killing. Nobody goes there now. Herman will never play there again."

"I told him to be honest with you," the father said, "but I'm worried about how this is going to affect him. He found a dead body. He tried to brag to his friends when he thought we couldn't hear. We put a stop to that."

"We'll be careful, Mr. and Mrs. de la Vega. We'll want to talk to him and all of his friends to learn as much as we can about that building."

The two detectives and the commander moved away from the parents.

"We got the rest of the kids who used the warehouse?" Fenwick asked.

"Yeah, we have a detail keeping them happy in the squad room," Poindexter said.

"Let's talk to junior finder first, then the rest of them," Turner said. "Do we have the preliminary reports on all of them?"

After glancing at the reports, they returned to the third floor. The kid who found the body sat in Fenwick's chair trying to bounce on the cushion long since flattened by Fenwick's substantial bottom. He must have been thirteen or fourteen. He watched the two cops walk toward him, his eyes alert. He grinned at them.

Any adult nonwitness or nonboss Fenwick would have roared at and unceremoniously dumped from the chair. Now he simply pulled another one over from the desk next to his. Turner grabbed the chair from behind his desk and brought it around to face the kid.

Herman de la Vega eagerly shook hands with the detectives.

"This is really cool," Herman said.

"Aren't you scared?" Fenwick asked.

"This is a police station," Herman said. "This is like television. I'm safe."

"How about when you found the body?" Turner asked.

The boy's face clouded. "It was awesome," he whispered. "I was a little scared, but I still looked. All my friends think it was really cool. I was really lucky. I'm glad they weren't with me. Now I'm a celebrity. If my parents let me, I think I can be on television."

Turner wanted to say all kinds of parental things about not playing in that kind of place and being careful, and make dire predictions about what could happen, but Herman was as close to a witness as they had so far. These cops would let Herman prattle on for hours. They might want to shut up Mrs. Bizerkowitz, but Herman could do anything short of reading aloud from the phone book and Turner and Fenwick would smile encouragingly.

"My mom and dad said you might arrest me for being in there.

I'm not going to get arrested, am I? I didn't do anything wrong."

Turner let the boy feel uncomfortable for a minute, then said, "You need to tell us all that you can. If you're honest, you won't be in trouble."

The boy nodded eagerly.

Turner asked, "How long have you been playing in that building?"

"We started going inside about two years ago. Nobody ever guards it. Sometimes homeless people sleep there. They try to chase us out sometimes. Once in a while we chase them. One of the gangs had it as a headquarters for a while so we couldn't play there. Then they found a better place, and we could go back."

"What happened last Friday?"

"A bunch of us were supposed to ditch school. I got away first."

"You ditch school often?"

"No. Once in a while. When it's too boring."

"So what happened?"

"Nobody else was there. The room where we usually hang out is way down the corridor and one floor up from the room the dead guy was in, but I could see the body from the hallway. I remember I was scared and I almost ran, but I called out and nobody answered and the body didn't move, so I figured the guy was dead. I didn't go in there. I ran for the cops."

"Did you see anybody in the street when you arrived?"

"Nope. There's no traffic around those buildings. That's why we play around there. Nobody bothers us."

"Did you notice anything unusual at all any time? Hear anything strange?"

"Nope. Just saw the body."

"How about in the last couple weeks? Seen any cars or trucks around the place? Anybody hanging around even last summer? An adult asking questions?"

The kid thought for a minute. "I can't remember that kind of thing. I for sure don't remember an adult asking us questions. I'd remember that."

"How about your friends?"

"I don't know. Probably not. They'd have said something, I think."

"We'll talk to each of them in a few minutes."

They assembled the kids outside a conference room in the rear of the fourth floor. Six kids, including Herman, sat eating dough-nuts at a six-foot brown folding table. Their chatter and activity hushed as the detectives neared them. Herman seemed to be pleased with his position as the one introducing the cops.

Three of the kids wore baseball caps turned backwards on their heads. They had on baggy pants over which they wore loose shirts that hung outside multicolored T-shirts draped to their knees. The smallest one of the group, Enrico, didn't wear a hat. He had his hair cut nearly bald on the sides but left an inch long and flat on top. He looked to be only twelve. He wore a junior wrestling champ T-shirt tucked into tight jeans. The other without a hat, Alfredo, snarled, grinned, or popped his gum while poking and punching his buddies. He reached for one guy's cap, but his hand got a lazy swat before it reached its destination. He was a trifle taller than the others and more heavyset. His T-shirt was taut over an ample belly, and the sleeves were too short for his arms. The cuffs of his ill-fitting jeans were frayed, the legs bunched against his sneakers, and his belly sagged over the waist. The back pocket flapped half off. His clothes seemed more hand-me-down and mismatched than trendy-grunge.

They took the kids one by one into the conference room. It differed from the all-gray interrogation room by having dull brown folding chairs, a larger dull brown table, and walls painted dull brown.

Turner explained to each one, "We need background informa-tion from you guys. We need your help to catch a killer."

The three with the caps weren't much help.

Enrico, the smallest one, immediately said, "He wasn't from around here."

"How do you know?"

"Everybody would talk about it. Everyone talks. We know

everything that goes on." He puffed out his chest in bold assertion.

"That so?" Fenwick asked.

"Yeah. And none of us is in a gang. But we hear. We know."

"How long have you guys been playing there?"

"We don't play, man, we hang out."

Turner found himself only half listening. His fatigue was catching up to him. He sat up straighter in his chair and concentrated.

"Some of us been hanging out there for five years," Enrico said. "I've been the longest. I'm fifteen now." Small for his age.

"What does hanging out mean?" Turner asked.

"We go there when our parents hassle us. Or just to be with our friends. Sometimes we get fries and soda pop if anybody's got any money. We don't do drugs or drink. We talk about our girlfriends. You know, hang out. We always use the back room you found. When we were little, we used to scare each other about getting up to our meeting room in the dark without a flashlight. Alfredo was the last one to finally do it. When the gangs were around a year ago, we had to be careful for a while."

"Why'd they leave?"

"It got too wrecked up even for them. We don't mind."

"Tell me about recently," Turner said. "Think of even the slightest thing unusual or out of the way at that place. Anything you saw, heard, or even thought you saw or heard."

Enrico frowned thoughtfully for several minutes.

"Anything?" Turner prompted.

Enrico said, "The street outside there is so quiet. The new guy fixing his place up says hello, but he works every night and doesn't hassle us. We get homeless in the winter sometimes, but it's too far from their territory. Too far to walk to where they get hand-outs or ask people for money, or from any of the missions."

After an hour of talking to the teenagers, the sum of the cops' increased knowledge added up to zero. Turner and Fenwick watched the group troop out.

Fenwick leaned back in his chair. "Is this day ever going to end?" he asked.

"Killer took a hell of a lot of chances," Turner said. "How did he know there weren't gang members, neighborhood kids, or a stray homeless derelict to accidentally interrupt him?"

"Maybe he wants to be caught, or is that just serial killers?"

"Or maybe he's been around for a long time and knows the area."

"Did we get that serial killer profile crap?"

Turner hunted on his desk. "I thought it was here."

"They all set fires and hurt furry little animals as kids. Don't look for it. Blessing'll have the details upstairs somewhere. I suppose we'll have to refresh our memories on that shit. Is this a serial killer?"

"I don't think two equals a serial killer."

"Thought I was going to fall asleep there for a few minutes," Fenwick said.

"I started wondering who was asking all those boring questions," Turner said. "Then I realized it was me." He rubbed the back of his neck. "I don't suppose we could just leave all this and run off to Canada for some fishing?"

The door to the conference room clicked open. Alfredo, the more heavyset teen, stuck his head in. He glanced over his shoulder and then around the room. He slipped inside, hunching himself near the doorway.

"What's happening, Alfredo?" Fenwick asked.

"Something strange."

The cops waited patiently.

"Last week Tuesday, early in the morning, I was there by myself. I slept overnight. Don't tell my parents, please?"

"If you help us, Alfredo, we'll help you," Fenwick promised.

"I was leaving early. Just before dawn. I saw this guy drive up. He got out of his car and began creeping around the back of the building. He came inside. He didn't see me. There's a million places to hide around there. He had a flashlight. He explored all over."

Alfredo stopped talking and stared at the top of his running shoes.

"Why didn't you tell us this the first time we talked to you?"

"The guys might have heard, or maybe they thought I'd be talking to you too much, but I want to catch the guy. If I help, will I be on television?"

"Tell me about the car," Turner said.

"Red, I think. It was dark."

"Dark red or too dark to tell what color it was?"

"Dark red."

"How about the man driving?"

"Bald on top. I could see the hole when he leaned over to get in the building. This big." Alfredo made a hole the size of a baseball with his fingers.

Turner watched Fenwick unconsciously finger the patch that had begun on the crown of his head six months ago.

Alfredo continued, "He didn't look real old. Maybe like you guys."

"Tall, short?" Fenwick asked.

"Maybe medium."

"What did you do?"

"As soon as I didn't hear his footsteps, I ran."

The detectives tried to jog his memory for another half hour, but got nowhere. Alfredo left.

Fenwick sighed. "Add one bald guy in a red car to the list. Only a few zillion of those on the planet."

The door opened. The sergeant from the desk downstairs said, "The guy from the sky box is here."

Turner and Fenwick shuffled down to the third-floor interrogation room.

Outside the door, Fenwick said, "He's the last one besides the players to see them alive. Maybe he'll remember something they said that could be important."

"I'm past tired on this."

"If he confesses, I'll kiss him."

"Hell, I'll marry him."

They were introduced to Daryl Logan. He wore a gray herringbone sport jacket with patches at the elbow. His shirt was light green and adorned by a white and gray paisley tie. He wore gray slacks and Gucci loafers. He had the slender frame of a runner who occasionally worked out as well. His brown hair was clipped short.

They sat in the room of gray walls, gray chairs, and gray table. Logan matched the decor perfectly.

"I'm a part-time professor and part-time administrator at St. Basil's University," he explained. "They divide up the use of the sky box among administrators, select faculty, and visiting dignitaries. It's used quite often to impress people in a position to donate to the school's endowment. College is big business these days."

"We understand you were in charge of the group that night," Turner said.

"I acted as more of a liaison. I arranged for the tickets before the game. In the sky box I was supposed to meet the needs, do the bidding of, keep happy, obey any commands. I want to move up the academic and administrative ladder. You need to know whose butt to kiss and when." He smiled. "I'm a realist."

"How did Jake Goldstein and Frank Douglas behave that night?"

"Polite, cheerful, unobtrusive. Didn't give me any trouble."

If he said they were saints, Turner thought he might throttle Daryl Logan on the spot. Turner found himself repeating by rote, "Did you notice anything at all odd or unusual?"

Daryl frowned as thoughtfully as anyone else they'd questioned in the last three days.

"They might have squabbled briefly about where to go after the game."

The detectives waited. Turner saw Fenwick's eyelids begin to droop.

"What'd you hear?" Turner asked.

"Not much. I think one wanted to go straight home after talking with the players. The other wanted to go somewhere. They saw I could hear and stopped talking. They weren't angry at each other, really. The Goldstein boy did say he needed to get home. This was at halftime. They seemed to laugh and cheer as much after as before their words. Didn't seem like much, but you asked for anything."

Turner probed some more, but when Daryl left fifteen minutes later the cops had nothing new.

Fenwick said, "I'm awake but not by much."

The watch commander came in and told them the owner of a small business across the street and down the block from the murder scene was at his place of business, if Turner and Fenwick wanted to talk to him.

Outside, the cool night air refreshed them a little. They traveled the few blocks to the neighborhood where the crime was committed. They cruised the front and side of the building they'd found the body in.

"Not a lot of street lights," Fenwick said.

"Back was actually better lit, but fortunately for our jobs plenty of shadows all around to park a car so that it wouldn't be noticed." They drove to the corner.

"This the only business operating around here?" Fenwick asked.

Turner flipped through a stack of papers. "Uniforms only listed this one."

They parked half a block down from the factory and banged on the door of a building on the opposite side of the street. Through pebbled-glass windows they could make out vague movements. Moments later the door was yanked open by a man in his early thirties.

After the cops introduced themselves, he invited them in. He was about five feet eight, but Turner thought he must eat steroids for breakfast, lunch, and dinner. He wasn't fat, but he was the most muscle-bound person Turner had ever seen. A paint-spattered T-shirt concealed muscles that strained the material all around his torso. The part of his upper arms Turner could see had veins easily observable crawling just underneath the rippling flesh. The guy's wheat-colored jeans clung to every inch of his lower body, revealing that he must either stuff his crotch with baseballs and socks or he was the most well-endowed man in history. His name was Drew Riley.

The room they were in had bare walls, a cement floor, a stack of paint cans on the left, and boards and bricks on the right.

"I'm fixing the place up," Riley said. He led them through a passage to a room with recently painted walls, bright orange carpeting, but no furniture. The entire place smelled of paint, new-sawn wood, and urban rot. "It's gonna take me a while. There's no place to sit really, but this room is the cleanest. Gonna be the hottest fitness center. All the yuppies are moving this way. I'm gonna cash in big time."

"You here a lot?"

"Yeah. That's what I told the uniformed cops who came to talk to me. I work at a health club on the north side and then I come here for eight to ten hours a day to work. I'm doing it all myself. Got the money for the down payment from an uncle who died. It's gonna be perfect. I can't put the pool in myself, but after I'm open a year, with all the new memberships, I'll be able to afford that."

"What happened Thursday night?"

"Oh, yeah. I had the game on a portable television upstairs. I was painting some rooms on the north side of the building. The side away from the street. I had an hour's worth of work left after the game got over, so I thought I'd stick it out. I put on the radio. The painting took longer than I thought. I came down here to use the john when I saw lights go by on the street. It's kind of rare when anybody comes down here at night. I thought it was a little odd. When I got back upstairs, I looked out the front window up there, since you can't see out these. I saw one of those little foreign cars with its brake lights on and the headlights off. He was just sitting there."

"You sure it was a he?"

Drew thought a minute. "I didn't see real clearly, but I thought it must have been a guy. Maybe I just assumed it was. I don't remember any longer hair that a woman might have."

"Was he alone?"

"It was one of those foreign jobbies. Only two seats in the front. I only saw one head."

"What'd he do?"

"Sat there. He didn't do anything, and there's not much worth breaking into around here. I've got a gun I keep in my toolbox. I've got a permit for it—the other cops already asked." He showed them a .22 target revolver and the permit. Riley resumed, "The guy in the car didn't do anything threatening, and I can take care of myself. I wasn't worried, so I went back to work. When I left, he was gone."

"What color was the car?"

"Yellow, I think, maybe tan. The light was dim. It looked sort of old."

"Could whoever it was have seen your car?"

"There's a side entrance I pull into. It's like a sort of garage. I've got the security cameras and everything working already. It's the first thing that I put in after I bought this place. I know the neighborhood is going to be perfect in a few years, but for now it's better to be safe."

"Could the person have seen your lights?"

"I was working in the back most of the night, so maybe not. This place is pretty big."

"Must get a little spooky."

"Nah. I got the security, I got the gun, I got no imagination." He shrugged.

"Must take a lot of money to get this kind of place moving."

"Mostly hard work. I started small. Buy only what I can afford. Do it a little bit at a time."

"You from the area?"

"Moved here a couple years ago. Saved my money for years. That plus what my uncle left me let me get started on this. When I'm finished, I'm going to make big bucks with this place."

"Have you seen a beat-up pickup truck around the neighborhood any time lately, or a dark red car?" Turner asked.

Riley thought for a few seconds. "Can't say I have. One of those the kind of car the killer had?"

"We don't know. We've only had descriptions of two vehicles so far. Yours is the third." Turner didn't add that none of them remotely matched.

"Just wanted to help as much as I could. Shame about those two kids. I hear they were saints."

Turner and Fenwick left. Fenwick said, "He gets run through the computer check just for that last remark if nothing else."

"Must have taken him years to bulk up like that."

"And half the steroids in the city. We got any more trips before we get back to the station?"

Turner riffled through his papers. "Nothing." He rubbed the back of his neck and then massaged his temples. "I don't want to think about how much sleep I haven't had."

"We're going to be getting even less if we don't get a break on this," Fenwick said. They returned to Area Ten headquarters to check the latest leads, fill out paperwork, and get depressed.

Around seven, Blessing called down on the interoffice line. "Why don't you guys stroll up here?"

They found Blessing with his hands rapidly tapping on computer keys. "I think we've got a lead on a possible witness." He motioned over a uniformed cop Turner and Fenwick didn't recognize. Blessing introduced her as Alice Drindle. "She's been handling the calls from people who used the parking garage. Tell them, Alice."

"I got a call about half an hour ago. This guy claims he saw something suspicious on Thursday night. I've had about a dozen people say that, but this guy was different. He seemed to know what he was talking about. He described the kids' van exactly."

"Where is he?" Fenwick demanded.

"Blessing said I should have him come in. He's on his way. I think he wants to be on television."

The detectives sighed.

"Everybody wants their fifteen minutes," Blessing said.

"Guy's name is Charles Edward Stuart."

At eight a dapper man in a navy blue business suit was escorted into the third-floor detective room. He had hair combed straight back off his forehead. He was barely over five feet five and didn't look to have an extra ounce of weight on his slender frame. Turner estimated the guy was somewhere between thirty-five and forty.

Charles Edward Stuart said, "I'm a musician with the symphony. I play cello. We had practice late Thursday night."

Turner and Fenwick had given him coffee and all the deference a possible break in the case merited. If he really had something, they might erect a statue to him.

"You parked on the fourth level of the parking garage?"

"Yes, I always do. It's usually much less crowded, but if I hadn't gotten there early Thursday, I might not have gotten a space. I deliberately stayed late practicing with some friends so I'd miss all the traffic from the sports events. I heard the call for help on the radio today."

"What did you see when you went to your car?" Fenwick asked.

Stuart described the boys' vehicle and then said, "I only saw their van, but no teenagers. As I drove out, I saw a man lurking in the shadows. Mine was the only car on that level besides theirs. I thought the van must be this man's, but he wasn't walking purposefully toward it. More looking around as if he were lost."

"What did he do?" Fenwick asked.

"When he saw me, I thought he ducked into the shadows. Of course, he could have been walking toward an exit in that direction, but would he be leaving his vehicle at that hour of the night? There were lots of parking spaces on the upper level by that time and I think the garage closes, doesn't it?"

"We'll have to check," Fenwick said.

"What did he look like?" Turner asked.

"Magnificently wavy black hair, with huge broad shoulders. His clothes were dark. I didn't see his face. He was very thin, built sort of athletically. Maybe I saw one of the boys themselves. I was told they were athletic. I almost didn't call, because I thought it was probably one of them."

"We're glad you called," Fenwick said.

"Have I helped?" Stuart asked.

"We'll let you know," Fenwick said.

"What do I say if the reporters question me?"

"I think we can find you a way to get out of here without having to run the press gauntlet," Fenwick said.

Stuart looked disappointed, but he allowed himself to be led to a back entrance where fewer press would be hovering. They told the uniformed cop escorting him to make sure Stuart got to his car without encountering any reporters.

"Neither of the kids had wavy black hair," Turner said.

"Sounded like Waverly, the football player," Fenwick said.

"Let's see if that computer check on him is back yet."

The background check on Waverly showed he had no outstanding arrest warrants, no unpaid parking tickets, and no hint of a connection to the murder.

"Where's he from?" Turner asked.

"Lives here," Fenwick said.

"No, I mean originally. There's gotta be more past history than this."

"We've got profiles started on lots of the people you've talked to," Blessing said. "That wouldn't be in police records. Holly's working on those. Wait." Blessing strode over to a uniformed cop's desk. He conferred with her for a moment and then brought over a sheet of paper. "Here's what we got on the team guys you talked to. The profile on Waverly says he attended college in Seattle at the University of Puget Sound, where he starred. Originally came from Spokane, Washington. Since he turned pro five years ago, he's played with four teams scattered around the country."

"He's not that good?" Fenwick asked.

"Good enough to catch on, but not good enough to stay long. Wonder if it's personality or ability that keeps him moving."

"Let's ask."

One of the uniformed cops tracked Waverly down on his car phone. He walked in half an hour later.

"Am I being arrested?" he asked.

"Did you do something you should be arrested for?" Fenwick asked.

"We just need to talk to you some more," Turner said.

Waverly sat in a chair next to Turner's desk. He crossed his arms over his chest and said, "I want my lawyer."

"We didn't arrest you. We didn't even tell you what we want to talk about. Why would you need a lawyer?"

"I won't answer any of your questions. I want my lawyer."

They tried numerous questions and subtle reasoning. They even gave good-cop bad-cop a shot. Nothing worked. Waverly simply demanded his lawyer.

This was a delicate area for the detectives. While certainly he wasn't being arrested and was barely a suspect, they wanted to ask him questions. That Waverly wouldn't answer questions wasn't supposed to incriminate him, but for Turner and Fenwick it added a host of suspicions.

They left Waverly sitting in the middle of the room while they conferred near the top of the stairs.

"What the hell is his problem?" Fenwick asked. "I'm tired enough to beat the shit out of him, but I suppose somebody would think that was unconstitutional. Double fuck."

They heard footsteps. Moments later Commander Poindexter marched up the steps to them. "I heard you have a suspect. What's going on? We got a killer here or what?"

Turner and Fenwick explained.

The commander shook his head. "He's a player from the team. They can afford lawyers, and they have publicity people out the wazoo. We've got to be careful."

"I don't give a shit about publicists," Fenwick said. "We've got two murders to solve. You've got at least as much pressure on this as we have."

"I know, but . . . ," Poindexter began.

Waverly walked up to the three of them. "I don't have to stay here," he said. "If I am not charged, I can leave. Either charge me, get me a lawyer, or I'm going home."

Waverly certainly showed none of the nervousness, fear, or confusion that Turner had learned to look for as signs that often pointed to someone who'd committed a crime.

An hour later a lawyer from the team sat with Waverly, Turner, and Fenwick in the interrogation room.

"We have a witness who places you in the parking garage about the time of the murder," Fenwick said.

"I wasn't there," Waverly said.

"Where did you go after the game?"

"Home."

"Anybody witness you arriving home?"

"No."

They sat silently for a minute.

Finally Fenwick demanded, "Why didn't you tell us that in the first place? We could have all gone home an hour ago."

"But you wouldn't have stopped there," Waverly said. "And we wouldn't have gone home. You wouldn't have let me leave with just those couple of questions."

And nothing further could they get from him. They wanted to hold him for a lineup then, but they couldn't get hold of the cello player from the symphony. The lineup would have to wait for the morning.

The commander told Fenwick and Turner to come in late the next morning. Detectives working on the brink of total exhaustion would be useless. He'd have given them the advice sooner, but the pressure for a suspect was as intense on him as it was on his people. Others would continue the work of the task force. The two detectives could pick up the threads when they came in. Turner and Fenwick agreed to meet at the funeral for the two boys at eleven the next morning at Holy Name Cathedral.

Turner drove up to his house at two. He switched off the car and listened to the motor click softly. The hall night light was on in his house. He could see the light was on in Mrs. Talucci's kitchen. She sat at her butcher-block table, a book in front of her.

She glanced up and saw him sitting in the car. She closed her book and rose from the table. Minutes later Paul saw the front porch light flip on. He eased himself out of his car. Tired as he was, he would stop and talk to Rose. No matter what the time or circumstance, she had always been there for him and his kids. He would talk to her now, even if she weren't dying.

He met her on the front porch. She held her robe closed at the throat.

Paul spoke quietly, "It's late, Rose. You should be in bed." The silent early morning street enveloped their words.

"So should you," she said. "I've got food. You look like you need it." Even Fenwick's prodigious appetite had given way to the needs of the case. Paul hadn't eaten since early this afternoon.

At her table, as had happened so many late nights before, he prepared to eat. He thought of all those times in the past and how few there would be in the future. He could not stop the moisture in his eyes.

He felt Rose's hand on his shoulder from behind. "Now is not the time for tears," she said. "Perhaps after I'm gone. Let's just talk now."

Paul wanted to ask her how she was feeling, what she'd done that day, what it felt like to know that she was going to die.

Instead, under her gentle probing he told about his day, his worries about the case. She listened quietly as she always did, her brown eyes watching his as he drank homemade soup and chewed on fresh, homemade bread.

At the end he said, "I think what bothers me most is missing Ben. I haven't seen him in two weeks. I want to talk to him, hold him. I know I should be more worried about the murder of those two boys, but I just want Ben."

"He was here," Rose said.

"Why?" Paul asked.

"He feels the same way about you. I suggested he stay in your house and wait for you. He's afraid if you didn't invite him, it might be awkward."

"He's stayed overnight before."

"But not without an invitation and not without you there. I knew it would be all right."

"It is."

"He watched Jeff early this evening and I believe he talked to Brian for quite a while. He loves you as much as you love him."

Paul felt a little less tired. "But I'm worn out. I need to get some sleep."

"He knows. He's probably asleep himself. It will be all right. You don't always have to speak volumes. Sometimes all you need to do is know the other is there."

Paul stood up. "What about you, Rose? Are you okay?"

"Of course. I've had a good life. I was in love for forty-eight years with a wonderful man. I have my family. I've had you and your boys. I've had more than enough love for one lifetime. Asking about my health now is nonsense. Go see Ben. He loves you very much."

Paul hugged Rose. He felt her thin frame under her robe. She patted him gently. He hurried to his own house. Ben lay fully clothed on the couch. The hall light illuminated half of his face. Paul watched him sleep for a few minutes. Paul loved the craggy lines of Ben's unhandsome face. The shadows seemed to make them more rugged than ever. He could picture Ben in front of a campfire out west, firelight flickering in the darkness. Paul started to cross the room. Ben stirred and opened his eyes.

"Paul?" Ben said.

"Yeah, it's me."

Ben staggered to his feet. He was groggy and half asleep. They held each other gently.

"I love you," Paul said.

He felt Ben's embrace tighten.

"We should go to bed," Paul said.

Ben nodded.

After checking on Jeff, Paul and Ben eased up the stairs together. Paul remembered to set the alarm as he undressed. He snuggled close to Ben, whose arm gently caressed him for a few minutes. Paul felt him slackening his movements, patting him, but he couldn't keep his own eyes open. He put his head on Ben's chest and fell asleep.

S I X

The next morning Paul woke up to a silent house. Usually the morning bustle of his two sons easily wakened him even if the alarm didn't. He realized Ben wasn't in bed next to him. The digital clock on the nightstand read 9:00 A.M. He threw on jeans, a sweatshirt, and gym socks and padded downstairs.

Ben sat at the kitchen table sipping coffee and reading the *Chicago Tribune*.

They exchanged good mornings. "Boys get off to school okay?" Paul asked.

"We were all very quiet. Figured you needed the sleep. I helped with breakfast. Jeff insisted that I tell you he loves you."

Paul squeezed Ben's shoulder as he passed by him to grab a mug from the cabinet and pour himself a cup of coffee.

"I'm glad you were here," Paul said. He still felt wiped out, but the few extra hours of sleep had helped. "Don't you have to be at the shop?"

"I'm the boss. I can do what I want. Besides, Myra is there. She's much tougher on the rest of them than I am."

"I've got to shower and get to the funeral by eleven."

"I'll make you breakfast."

"You don't have to . . . "

"I want to."

After letting water cascade over his body for fifteen minutes, and then a meal of fresh fruit, bacon, eggs, and potatoes, without an excessive amount of fresh vegetables, Paul felt more awake than he had in days. The phone rang as he was drinking an extra cup of coffee.

It was Ian. "Why didn't you tell me these were homosexual murders?" Ian demanded by way of hello.

"What homosexual murders? I thought we didn't. . . ."

"I know we don't say 'homosexual murders,' but two of the Chicago morning television shows are reporting that Goldstein and Douglas died because of some gay connection, only they used that bullshit 'homosexual murder' tag. As if some goddamn heterosexual couldn't leave a string of dead males. Jesus fucking Christ, I am pissed!"

Turner sighed. He hated the term "homosexual murder." Did it mean that a homosexual was committing murders or that homosexuals were being murdered? He hated the clinical sound and the inherent homophobia of too many who used the term.

Turner said, "As far as I know, the murders aren't gay-related."

"Well, you better talk to the police department public relations division. They were quoted."

"Shit."

"An excellent reaction and an accurate description."

"What'd the reports say?"

"Quoted some guy who claims he saw the boys at a gay bar. You know how loony some people around this town get if they think there's a gay connection. After Gacy and Eyler, you'd think they'd learn better."

"This is the first I've heard about their sexuality having anything to do with the murder. We have no evidence from the scenes of sexual activity. Both boys have solid heterosexual credentials. It's usually the kids from poor families, history of drugs, whatever, who the Gacys and Eylers go after. You know the drill. Boys out there hustling for money, drugs, or kicks. None of that fits the profile of these kids or any of the facts that we've been able to find."

"Well, you've got it now."

"You remember the name of the guy who gave the interview?"

"Yeah. Claimed he was Purple Steve, a bartender at the Leather Strap. Somebody at Area Ten will have the details by the time you get there. What are you doing home? I called headquarters first."

"Trying to get some sleep. I'm going to the funeral in a few minutes."

"Maybe I'll stop by the station later. I'm trying to get information on Purple Steve. I'd like to blow his bubble or get an exclusive with him. He sounded like a jerk."

"We need all the useless leads we can get."

"You sound as if you could use a lot more sleep," Ian said. "Let's try and get together for dinner tonight."

"Dinner sounds real iffy. Call me later."

Paul told Ben about the latest development.

"Only makes it tougher," Ben said. "You gonna make the game tomorrow night?"

They'd planned on going to the Bulls game for months. The tickets had been a gift from Mrs. Talucci for Paul and Ben's first anniversary of dating.

"I doubt if I'll be able to make it. I know we've been counting on it, but I'll make it up to you. Whether we go to the game or not, why don't you stay tonight? If there's any chance I can get away, I will."

Turner called Blessing. "What the hell's going on?"

"Place is nuts. Carruthers suggested we arrest Purple Steve. Rodriguez dragged Carruthers out of the station. You'll have to talk to Purple Steve."

"Yeah. I'm looking forward to it. Did they do the lineup on Waverly yet?"

"Yeah, guess what?"

"He picked out the wrong guy."

"Got it in one."

"Rats."

"Or as Fenwick would say, triple shit." Blessing chuckled.

Turner told Blessing they'd be in after the funeral and hung up.

Paul and Ben walked out to the car together. They saw Mrs. Talucci working in her garden. She was on her hands and knees replanting and rearranging her annual beds. She waved to them with a glove-covered hand. They strolled over.

As she stood up, Paul reached out a hand to her. She gently waved him away. She smiled at them both and pointed her trowel first at one, then the other. "That's the way you two should be. Together." Rose had been pushing their relationship shamelessly for years. Both men blushed slightly.

"You need any help, Rose?" Paul asked. "I could send Brian over after school."

"Bah. I already took care of it. He'll be here carrying boxes of dirt, fertilizer, and bulbs for an hour or two. I'll dig and shove and push dirt, but I gave up that carrying nonsense years ago."

Paul and Ben hugged in Mrs. Talucci's front yard. Paul felt himself smiling as he climbed into his car and drove away.

Turner parked next to a police barricade a half a block south of Holy Name Cathedral on State Street. A pleasantly cool breeze drifted in from the southwest. Turner found Fenwick slouched against a blue and white across from the cathedral steps.

"Heard about our latest lead?" Turner asked.

"We need that kind of crap," Fenwick said.

"Somebody getting pictures of the crowd?"

"Yeah." Fenwick pointed to two plainclothes detectives mingling with the camera crews from the television stations. Each cop sported a hand-held video recorder. "Probably won't do much good. The church is jammed. Probably be an overflow out here. Even if our killer shows up, he'll be totally lost in this mob." It was possible for the killer to be somewhere in the throng. The detectives also wanted to observe the families and close friends of the victims. As unlikely as it seemed, that was where a murderer was most likely to come from.

The detectives found their way into the cathedral through a side door reserved for dignitaries. They wound up standing in back. The nave was filled with students from the Kenitkamette High School, the families of the victims, and most of the political notables in the city. Mr. Goldstein had been a major part of the city for a long time. Turner thought he got a glimpse of Mayor Daley, Cardinal Bernadin, Governor Edgar, and Lou Holtz sitting in one of the front pews.

Numerous people gave eulogies. Bob Talbot, the hulk who was Jake and Frank's best friend on the football team, seemed to dwarf the rostrum when he spoke. Halfway through, he broke down sobbing as he had when they interviewed him. The kid had to be led away.

Their football coach began, "This is the saddest day of my life." When he got to the part about how perfect the boys were, Turner heard Fenwick groan softly.

As they began to roll the coffins down the center aisle, Fenwick leaned over to Turner: "Nobody confessed from the pulpit."

"Not today," Turner responded.

A uniformed cop slipped up next to them and whispered in Fenwick's ear. His partner beckoned for Turner to follow.

Once they were outside, Turner asked, "What's up?"

"Purple Steve is in the station ready for us."

After their first glance at him, they didn't have to wonder why he was called Purple Steve. He wore shirts, pants, shoes, and socks in various shades of purple.

"Guy looks like a giant grape," Turner muttered.

Fenwick said, "I'll stomp his ass to shit if the double fuck gives us any shit. He's gonna be one sorry fucker if he's lying to us."

They sat at their desks, chairs turned to face Purple Steve, who after some reluctance gave his last name as Smith.

Turner could see Roosevelt and Wilson sitting at their desk ten feet behind Steve Smith. Both wore solemn expressions that came closer to making Turner burst into hysterical laughter than if they'd been making faces and acting silly.

"You work where?"

"At the Leather Strap. You've probably never heard of it. It's a fabulous gay bar on the north side. In the gay part of town. Where you used to harass us."

Steve Smith must have been in his early twenties. Turner assumed no bar would be stupid enough to employ someone underage to serve drinks, but the guy was slender and baby-faced and looked very young. Turner knew the bar's reputation in the community, but he'd never been inside. Word was that no matter what its current incarnation—as disco bar, sports palace, or leather dungeon—you could always get drugs or a prostitute.

"I used to dance at the bar, but I gave that up and decided serving drinks had more dignity."

"Tell us about seeing Goldstein and Douglas."

"Well, I heard they were such cute boys, but I missed the first news reports and I didn't see any pictures. Then they had that special about Coach Goldstein on the news last night. It was my day off, so I watched. I saw the home movies of his kid playing some sport. I don't follow sports much. Silly nonsense getting all sweaty for nothing. When I saw the son and his friend in one part of the clip, I was sure I'd seen them on the dance floor of the bar."

"When?"

"That night."

"What time that night?"

"Before the murder."

"What time that night?" This time Fenwick growled the question.

Smith hesitated. "After eleven."

Turner suspected the guy was lying. His answer seemed more

like a guess than a statement, as if he'd picked a time out of the air and been lucky enough to choose a moment the boys might possibly have been there.

"They were only seventeen. How'd they get in the bar?" Fenwick asked.

"Talk to the doormen. Once they get past them, I figure it's okay to serve them. They're supposed to be the ones who check IDs."

"What did they do there?"

"Dance. It is a dance bar."

"When did they leave?" Fenwick asked.

"I only saw them the once for a brief minute."

Purple Steve left to shine in front of the reporters.

They'd have to question every employee of the place. A whole new set of possible witnesses. They trudged up to the fourth floor. They assigned personnel to the task and would plod up to the bar to do some of the questioning themselves later on. Turner asked Blessing for the latest reports and information. They read and filled out more papers, and wrote the daily update on their activities for the commander.

They spent three hours late that afternoon talking to people at the Leather Strap. Not a one had the slightest knowledge of or was willing to admit to seeing Goldstein or Douglas at the bar. They assigned two uniforms to wait out the night, asking all the patrons who came in if they had seen the boys. Turner suspected it would be a slow night at the bar. The blatant presence of cops asking questions wasn't likely to draw a crowd to a gay establishment.

As soon as they walked back into Area Ten headquarters, the uniform at the desk said, "Commander wants to see you. Half the brass in the city is here. You guys are in trouble."

They found the commander and the others in the open space in front of the floor-to-ceiling corkboard on the fourth floor. Turner recognized most of the assembled crowd: the assistant deputy superintendent of the entire department, the press relations maven, the director of Research and Development, the commander of the Communications Division, and the deputy superintendent of Technical Services. What most of them were doing here he soon found out.

The brass sat and questioned the commander and the two detectives relentlessly for over an hour. Turner and Fenwick might have excellent reputations in the department, but often you're only as good as your last case. The reward for good work is frequently the expectation of even more good work. The presumption of perfection on the part of superiors can have a demoralizing effect on the hardest working of detectives.

"Have you followed up every lead?" asked the deputy superintendent of Technical Services. It was the third time in the last ten minutes he'd asked the question.

"Which lead is it that you think we haven't followed up on sufficiently?" Turner asked. His voice was icily calm but on the correct side of polite to one of the brass.

"Well," the tubby little man blustered. He glanced at the others around the room. He grabbed at the stack of reports in front of him. "Well." He rapidly riffled through them. Finally he stuck on one. "What about this?"

Fenwick grabbed it. "This is a report from the western suburbs that says a kid at a fast-food restaurant claims he saw them yesterday morning having breakfast. That's Sunday. He claims he saw the kids after they were dead! Why in holy fucking hell should we follow up that kind of nonsense?"

"You have to follow up everything."

"Are you out of your fucking mind?"

"I don't have to stand for this." The tubby little man rose to his feet. "This department's been under a lot of pressure to solve this crime. It's your fault it hasn't been solved."

Fenwick banged his fist down on the desk. "Our fault! We aren't the fucking criminals here. How the glory-holy fuck are we supposed to investigate this bullshit? We've checked through the remotest possible lead seventeen times. Every person in the task force has been working nearly twenty hours a day. I don't give a royal-holy fuck how much pressure you've been under. I don't care if the pope and the king of the universe called. We ain't got shit, and each new lead piles on another avalanche of crap to the blizzard of paperwork we're already drowning under!" He banged his fist on the table again. "Our fault! If anybody has something constructive to say, I'm willing to listen. Until then. . . ."

Fenwick drew a deep breath.

The room had fallen deathly silent. In the past Fenwick had always stopped just before this kind of explosion, and now he'd done it with half the brass in the city looking on.

The deputy superintendent of Technical Services stepped back several paces from the conference table and openly gaped at Fenwick.

Commander Poindexter said to Turner, "Get him out of here."

Turner stood up. "Why don't we step into the office in back?" he asked softly.

Fenwick glared at the assemblage. His florid face had dangerous purplish tinges at numerous points.

"Come on, Buck," Turner said softly.

The other members of the group remained silent as Turner led Fenwick away. They crossed to the fourth-floor conference room surrounded by the quiet of the members of the task force, all of whom had witnessed an outburst most of them wished they had the nerve to make.

Fenwick entered, sat down on one of the metal folding chairs, propped his elbows on the desk, and rubbed his fingers against his eyes. "Double fuck and triple fuck," he said quietly.

Turner knew that the highest rating anyone could get in Fenwick's system was "triple fuck." Usually he reserved this sacred category for inept Bears quarterbacks when they threw game-losing interceptions, or Cubs pitchers who walked in winning runs. The system proceeded through three levels of "shit" to the highest "fuck" category. It was a perfect sign of Fenwick's fury.

"And don't tell me I fucked up, Paul. I know I fucked up." He clasped his hands behind his head, leaned back in the chair, and shut his eyes.

A few minutes later the commander joined them. "Never

thought you'd really do that in front of this kind of gathering," he said.

Fenwick sat up in the chair. "Guy deserved it," he said.

"That may be so, but he's a boss. I calmed him down a little before I got in here."

Turner leaned his back up against the door. He jammed his hands in his pants pockets. The commander perched on the edge of the desk.

"I agree with Buck," Turner said.

"I've never pushed harder on a case," the commander said. "Everyone has worked too hard. I can try and placate the guy you insulted. Although I'm sure Stuart O'Dell, the guy in charge of Technical Services, is probably on the phone to the Superintendent even as we speak, declaring your evils to that august personage."

"Screw it," Fenwick said. "It's done. We've got more important shit to do than worry about any of those assholes." He sighed. "If the killer walked in right now, I'd kiss him," he said.

Someone knocked on the door and a second later a uniformed cop stuck his head in the room. "Sorry to interrupt, Commander. The Superintendent is on the phone."

Turner and Fenwick trudged down to the third floor and sat at their regular desks. The squad room was unnaturally quiet. Turner noticed people avoided looking directly at Fenwick. News traveled fast in the small world of Area Ten headquarters.

Turner rubbed his hands across his face. He felt the strain in every muscle when he moved. The phone on Turner's desk rang. He cradled it on his shoulder and managed a civil hello.

It was Ian. "Catch you at a bad time?"

"Every time is bad these days. What can I do for you?"

"You sound like you need a break. I can take you to dinner in half an hour. I've got information on Purple Steve. I'll be right down. You've got to eat sometime. I don't care how badly the criminals of Chicago want you."

Turner called home. Jeff answered. "Ben said he'd take us out to dinner. Are you coming home? He said we'd have to wait for you to decide. I like Ben. Are you coming home? Brian wants permission to go out."

Paul talked to both of his sons, giving assurances or permission as appropriate or called for. To Ben he said, "I can cancel a dinner I've got."

"Don't. It's okay. The boys and I will shift for ourselves. I'm going to take them out to a little Italian place I know. We'll be fine. Get home when you can."

Paul thanked him and hung up.

Fenwick chose to stop at home. They tentatively agreed to meet back at the station later that evening.

Ian entertained Turner with newspaper gossip as they drove to Genessee Depot, one of Ian's favorite eating spots on the north side. They sat in a booth near the window so they could look out. The unhurried atmosphere and the classical music playing softly soothed Turner's nerves.

The meal passed mostly in silence. Ian recognized that what his friend needed was companionship. When dessert arrived, Ian announced, "The Goldstein and Douglas deaths have no connection to being gay."

"I agree."

"Did you talk to Purple Steve?"

"We did. Who is that jerk?"

"He has a Ph.D. in philosophy from either Yale or Harvard. I forget which. Besides working part time at the Leather Strap, he answers the phones at some sleazy hotel on Halsted Street. It's an establishment that caters to the lost and lonely. A hustler hotel."

"How nice for him. He was trying to hustle the cops and the media for his fifteen minutes of fame. He'll be lucky if we don't run his ass in. Fenwick may simply ram Steve's head through the nearest wall if he ever sees him again."

"Probably wouldn't hurt Steve near enough."

"Nobody else who works there saw the kids. The bouncer insists he never lets anyone in who's underage."

"That may actually be true. Lately the vice division of your department has been hanging around there. They've had to be careful. I interviewed Purple Steve."

"And now you're best friends?"

"At first he claimed every word he told the cops was true, but I'm a wily old reporter. I dig out little secrets. Seems our buddy Steve Smith has an outstanding prostitution warrant from another jurisdiction."

"You're making this up?"

"Nary a word."

"How did you find out?"

"Sources."

"So you know something rotten about him?"

"I mentioned it to him. Told him if he didn't come clean, I would announce that little fact to every media outlet in the city and to every cop I could get my hands on. At that point the truth slipped from his lips. The dumb shit made it all up."

"If I had the energy, I'd have him arrested. If I see his face on another television station, I will have him arrested. I may anyway."

"Be my guest."

"Even if it means breaking a trust and giving up a source?"

"He's not a source. He's a poor asshole who screwed up big time. If stupidity is a crime, he's guilty."

"He wasted a lot of people's time today."

"So. Lock him up."

"Not at the moment."

Turner told his friend about the case. He wasn't worried about giving privileged information to Ian. His friend knew how to keep his mouth shut, and he was an ex-cop. Ian might have insights they'd missed. Turner trusted Ian's instincts.

"That stuff about crushed testicles is odd," Ian said. "You know that gay suicide stuff I've been working on?"

Turner nodded.

"Remember, I told you about the interview I was going to have with that woman from Spokane, Washington? I mentioned it the night I baby-sat."

1 1 6

"Yeah, you said you were having breakfast with the coroner or something."

"Assistant deputy coroner who helped with the autopsy."

"Right, whatever."

"I try and track all those kinds of things down. Trouble is, most of the time the family won't talk, and I wouldn't want to bother them at such an awful moment. That's trash journalism. Usually I can't get the officials to tell me much either."

"So what did this one tell you?" Turner asked.

"I think I've got the start of something. The kid was one of the biggest sports heroes ever to hit town. This was maybe nine years ago. It made the national papers. She was really good to talk to. First time I've got an official who dealt with that kind of case to open up to me. She told me that no one could figure out why he'd want to commit suicide and that she was sure this kid didn't kill himself."

"No? How'd they figure that out? Wasn't there a note or something?"

"She told me the cops said there was a lot of depressing poetry the kid wrote. Everybody figured a sports kid who wrote poems had to be gay, but nobody in the press reported that. The woman I talked to found something really strange. She wouldn't tell me anything over the phone at the time without a release from the family."

"Did she succumb to your fatal charm in person?"

"No, she quit her job and was going to work someplace else. Denver, I think. I found out she was a lesbian and we knew people each other knew in several activist causes."

"So what did you learn?"

"The kid had been hanged, but they also found his dick and balls had been crushed as if they'd been pulverized with a baseball bat. The killer did it after he strung him up. It was murder."

"Did she report that at the time?"

"Her bosses and the family didn't want to hear about it, but the cops looked into it. They never found a suspect or probable cause or anything. They wrapped it up as a suicide and let it go."

"You saying this is the same killer?"

"All I know for sure is that it's not going to help my suicide theory or get me any closer to writing a Pulitzer Prize article on gay suicide, but as a cop, do you believe in coincidences?"

"No, but your killing was nine years ago."

Ian said, "I don't believe in coincidences. These have to be connected. Maybe there were others."

"Other what?"

"Kids who were sports stars killed under unusual circumstances."

"Who all got their nuts crushed? I wouldn't want to be the one to bring that theory up to my boss. Although this one is better than the total zero we have now. But your dead guy was in Spokane years ago. This is Chicago, today. That's a hell of a stretch. Why'd the killer move?"

"Gee, gosh, not to get caught?"

"Sarcasm does not become you. You're losing it, Ian. A serial killer after star sports kids? Who roams around the country?"

"Serial killers move around. It's part of the profile."

"This is a serial killer? I have my doubts."

"How many cop hours did you waste on Purple Steve?"

"Too many."

"This has more possibilities than that."

"Not by much. Does your theory really make sense to you?"

"Nothing about this killing makes sense, but if it was random violence, it was well-planned random violence. You haven't been able to get any angle on why these two kids would be killed. No one has a motive. Nothing you've found in their lives leads to somebody killing them. No one they knew had a motive. You keep coming up with nothing, because there is nothing. This at least would be something."

"Wouldn't somebody have noticed if there were an unusual number of deaths of kids who were sports stars?" Turner asked.

"I don't know," Ian said, "and neither do you, but if you don't follow it up, and later it turns out to be true?"

"You'll never let me hear the end of it." Turner paused. "It could be true. We are desperate for leads."

"Maybe I'll get that Pulitzer after all," Ian said.

"Maybe you'll get your butt in gear and help us with the research." Turner stood up.

"Where are you going?"

"I'm going to check it out."

"How? It's eight o'clock. What are you planning to check?"

"If other sports stars have died."

"And if their balls have been crushed? Would most places know that?"

"I'll find out," Turner said.

Turner called Fenwick at home from a pay phone. His partner was as skeptical as he but willing to listen and to help do research.

Fenwick met Ian and Turner on the fourth floor of Area Ten headquarters half an hour later.

Turner was halfway through his explanation to Blessing when the young cop held up his hand, "Already done."

"Huh?" Turner said.

"Routine in this kind of thing. One of the first things I did when we got all the computer stuff hooked up was get into the NCAVC and VICAP. Too many cops wait too long to get into those systems."

NCAVC was the National Center for the Analysis of Violent Crime and VICAP the Violent Criminal Apprehension Program. Both were under the aegis of the FBI. Any police department could feed in data or use the data that was stored in the system to help them solve crimes committed in their jurisdiction.

"So what did they say?" Fenwick asked.

"We got no match in method of operation. What we've got here is fairly unique."

"What about testicles being crushed?" Turner asked.

"I sent that through. Let me check." He tapped computer keys for half a minute. "No crushed testicles," Blessing said.

"Must not be a common method of execution for serial killers," Turner said.

"I still think it's a possibility," Ian said.

Fenwick said, "It's not something they're going to look for. The one you had, Ian, was from before they began to set up the system. And you only found out because you had a connection. I bet there are others. There have got to be others."

"You'd have to do the research on your own," Blessing said. "Do you know how many teenagers die each year in this country?"

"No," Turner admitted.

"Thousands. You can't eliminate suicides or accidents from any search, because the killer might have disguised them. It would take forever."

"Got to start somewhere," Ian said.

"I'll help for a while," Turner said, "but if we don't turn up something quickly. . . ."

Blessing sighed. "We can get some of the newspapers on computer, but for background research you'll have to do it yourself."

Ian suggested the main branch of the Chicago Public Library as the most likely to have national newspapers on file. At nine o'clock they rode over. They entered by a side entrance and presented their identification to the head of security, who agreed to let them in.

They walked across terrazzo floors and strode up silent escalators. Turner thought the maple wood used throughout made it seem like the library he'd used as a kid. At the periodicals desk on the third floor, Turner said, "We need to check the national news and the sports sections of each of these papers." He took the *New York Times,* Ian the *Chicago Tribune,* and Fenwick *USA Today.*

"Where do we start?" Fenwick asked.

"With the most recent and work back," Ian said. "Any time you find something with a sports star killed, make several copies of it." One of the security guards showed them how to use the machines.

"We should copy everything that has something to do with

teenagers dying under accidental or unexplained circumstances," Turner said. "Maybe they won't list stuff about playing sports."

"Okay," Ian said.

"It'll take forever," Turner said.

"If necessary, we can get an army of cops in here and find every teenage killing this century," Fenwick said.

After an hour the newsprint that whirled by began to blur together. Turner had to force himself to concentrate. Eventually he got into a rhythm of where to look in the *Times,* but by eleven he was exhausted. He managed to get the security guards to unbend enough to let them bring coffee up to where they were working.

At eleven-thirty the three of them met at one of the blond wooden tables. Fenwick's stack of copies was the largest.

"These state-by-state national pages have a few dead teenager things, but mostly accidents," Fenwick said. "I have fifteen of those, but I've only gone back three years. From the sports pages I have three reports, one last year and two from two years ago." He gave them the copies.

"We have any that match what Fenwick has?" Turner asked.

Before leafing through their stacks of materials, they arranged all of what they had by date. Then they tried cross-matching.

"What are we looking for?" Ian asked.

"A cluster of items that look suspicious," Turner said.

Ian said, "But if the killer made the one in Spokane look like a suicide, maybe he or she is clever enough to make all of them look like suicides or even accidents. How can you possibly find out if they're murders at this point?"

"Whichever one of us is the biggest fairy gets to wave the magic wand," Turner said.

"Leaving me out is discrimination," Fenwick said.

"Everybody kept all accidents and suicides?" Turner asked.

They all nodded.

"Let's see if we can get any kind of pattern or grouping besides chronological," Turner said.

They made three copies of their findings so each one had a

stack of items to hunt through. For fifteen minutes they perused their separate stacks. Finally Turner looked up. "This is goofy. You've just got a list of dead teenagers. You're not going to get a pattern. These papers would never have all the deaths we'd need to check. In this state alone there's a zillion little local papers to hunt through."

"A prominent athlete would be noticed," Ian said.

"This is useless," Turner said.

"You remember what the last tip we got was before Purple Steve?" Fenwick asked.

Turner nodded.

Ian shook his head. "What?"

"It took four cops all afternoon to check. Call came from O'Hare Airport. Some obscure high school sport team was passing through the city for some playoffs in Peoria. Somebody reported one of the kids missing and a suspicious passenger on the plane. We had to track the passengers, half the employees of the airline and the airport, and my great aunt Matilda. The suspicious guy turned out to look like an unreconstructed hippie who was a rocket scientist who has been in Russia for the past three years. They found the kid still mostly drunk but working on becoming very hung over back in East Nowhere, Iowa. What we've got here has at least as much possibility as that did of making a connection. We can't abandon it."

"Maybe we haven't gone back far enough," Turner said. "I'm willing to keep looking for a while longer."

Fenwick nodded.

"Although we could leave this for uniformed cops to compile," Turner said.

"I'm staying," Ian said.

They returned to work.

Just after 1:00 A.M. Fenwick's bellow broke the silence. Turner hurried down the aisle to see what was up. He met Ian and Fenwick at the end of a row of periodicals.

Fenwick was waving a piece of paper in his hand. "I've got it," he said.

"It better be pretty goddamn mind-boggling at this point," Turner said.

"Two sports stars in Tucson, Arizona, back six years ago. Look."

They read the article.

"There was a follow-up," Fenwick said. "There wasn't with most of these." He showed them the next article.

There had been a traffic accident, at first reported as two athletes coming home from a party, probably drunk, who had driven off a dark country road in the mountains. The follow-up article said that one of their friends had come forward after a week and admitted he'd followed his buddies with his lights off. He was going to sneak up on them and use his dad's volunteer fire department emergency lights to scare the hell out of them. Before he could catch up, he'd seen a car trying to shove the other vehicle off the side of the road. He'd witnessed his buddies' car fly off the road, plunge down the hillside, and burst into flames. He too had been drunk from the teenage trysting in the hills above the city, but had quickly become sober and very frightened. He was afraid the other car might be waiting and that he too might be run off the road. He'd been afraid to come forward, thinking that he might be blamed or get in trouble for being at the party, for which he'd been grounded from going.

The cops had tended to discount the boy's story, but they examined the burned and wrecked vehicle again. It was impossible to determine whether any of the cracks and dents on the boys' car had come from the plunge or from being side-swiped. But an enterprising young Tucson cop had found an abandoned car that had been reported stolen. The car had slender lines of paint that could have come from side-swiping another vehicle. A quick check showed them to be the same color as the car that had crashed and burned. The abandoned car had been reported stolen in Phoenix a week before the crash. The owner of the vehicle had over three hundred witnesses to where he was on the night of the accident. No suspect had been apprehended.

123

"No crushed nuts," Turner said. "You really think this is connected?"

"Compared to the leads we've gotten on some cases, this is fabulous," Fenwick said. "Did you look at some of the calls we've gotten on this case? One claimed Goldstein and Douglas were murdered by aliens from Mars who came to Earth to eat the livers of teenagers."

"I thought the teenage-liver-eaters came from Venus." Turner held up his hand to forestall his protests. " 'Tucson Teens Murdered' is a lovely headline, but I don't see much of a connection here."

"Waverly, the football player, was from Spokane," Fenwick said.

"So are lots of people," Turner said. "Doesn't mean they're killers, but we better run a complete profile on this guy. If he lived in Tucson. . . ."

"I want to talk to these people," Fenwick said. "The kid, the cops, the Medical Examiner. Everything."

"They're all in bed by now," Ian said, "or does their sleep get to be ruined?"

"You're usually out haunting bars well past this hour," Turner said.

"Investigative journalism," Ian said.

"Amazing what you can find attached to a beer bottle," Turner said.

"If it's handsome and delectable, it's in-depth research."

Fenwick said, "We can assign people to keep looking through these, plus we should try and match up anything else we found in the last couple hours. I, however, am not going to pursue it tonight. I'm going to get a few hours' sleep. We need more than just us on this."

"Do we have something?" Ian asked.

"I sure as hell hope so," Turner said.

Paul enjoyed the fact that he could go home and crawl into bed next to Ben. His lover woke briefly as Paul joined him.

Four hours later Paul awoke from the alarm more energetically than he had any time since the case began. He even found Brian's broccoli and cauliflower omelet edible. His elder son had been on a health-food kick since he read in an article that one of his sports heroes ate ten different helpings of vegetables a day. Paul balked at the fried zucchini that accompanied the omelet, but his sons devoured all of it. He saw them off to school, talked with Ben for a few minutes, grabbed a large-scale map of the United States from Jeff's room, and rushed to work.

He found Fenwick in the task force room pinning a huge map of the United States to the floor-to-ceiling corkboard. Turner showed his to Fenwick.

"Great minds run in the same rut," Fenwick said.

Turner pulled a package of multicolored pins out of his sport coat pocket. He took the sheaf of papers they'd found last night out of his briefcase. "Let's get somebody to put these on the locations of everything we found last night. As the information comes in, we can pin each city. Might make a pattern."

The commander entered the room. His shoulders sagged and it seemed to take a great effort for him to get his coffee cup to his lips for a brief sip. "What now?"

Turner and Fenwick explained their idea.

"Not only that," Turner said, "we can get each incident on computer. We'll be able to cross-match them easier that way. We can set up a grid by part of the country, city, type of accident, types of injuries, sports kids involved, kind of sport, everything, color of eyes of victims, whatever. When we talk to the different departments we can get any suspicions, anomalies, quirks, and then we can try and check autopsy reports. I'd like to talk to witnesses. Members of the family if possible. We can begin cross-matching all the data. If there's a serial killer out there, maybe we can find a pattern."

"Sounds kind of off the wall to me," the commander said.

"Better than some of the other crap we have," Fenwick said.

"Take forever," the commander said.

Fenwick glanced at the people slowly filtering into the office.

"We've had nearly seventy-five people running around this city like chickens with their heads cut off. Many on crap lots more impossible than this. We've got computers. We've got communications. I think we can get this stuff."

"You can get it," the commander said, "but will it do any good?"

"I think the testicles of the dead kid here and in Spokane being crushed has real possibilities," Turner said. "It could be the same killer." He repeated Ian's warning of the night before: "If it is the same killer, and we ignore it now, we're in for criticism later."

Fenwick added, "And if we're right, we look great."

The commander sipped coffee. "Okay, for a while. Go with it for forty-eight hours. If nothing comes of it by then, drop it, and don't put everybody on this. Keep following up any leads in this area at the same time." He sipped more coffee. "Buck, I talked to the Superintendent about you yesterday. Mr. O'Dell did call him."

"It's only good news if I've been fired."

"No such luck. You'll be around to work on lots more cases, but you've made a mortal enemy of Stuart O'Dell."

"What's he going to do? Slap me with a regulation?"

"He's a bureaucrat. He'll do something mean and nasty and probably sneaky to get revenge. I'd watch my back if I were you."

Fenwick nodded. He'd been around long enough to know that a direct assault from an enemy in the police department was unlikely. Nothing to do for now but get on with the job.

They dispatched fifteen people to the library to collect more data. They assigned twenty people to begin making follow-up calls. Turner and Fenwick rearranged work assignments on the chart next to their desk on the third floor. Twelve people were at computer terminals on the fourth floor. They sent six uniforms to police headquarters at 11th and State to pick up more hardware. By ten, not counting the people handling the routine calls for the task force, they had 75 percent of their people working on some aspect of the new lead. At eleven, a contingent returned from the library. They had expanded the search to other national newspapers. They dumped boxes of copies. More people were assigned to arrange them by date and area of the country. They sent out for more pins to be set into cities and towns on the huge map.

Task force members took the basic data and typed the details of each incident onto the computers, using the forty-two categories that Turner and Fenwick had agreed on with Blessing.

Between ordering the task force in this new direction, Turner and Fenwick began to make calls on the most likely cases. Turner called the county coroner for Tucson, Arizona, at 9:30 A.M. Arizona time. She remembered the case clearly.

"One of the boys was burned beyond recognition," she said. "The other was thrown from the car, which then rolled over him and set him on fire. Crushed all the bones on the right side of his body."

"I've got kind of a strange question." Turner explained the murder they were working on and the anomaly of the testicles of one of the boys being crushed and the lack of underwear on the victim.

"I think I'd remember that," she said. "Although, honestly, I don't know if we checked. It was pretty obvious what killed both boys. Wouldn't the killer have had to park, walk down the mountain, do his dirty work, and get back up, risking somebody seeing him hanging around the crash or especially the fire?"

"At the moment it's the only lead I've got," Turner said.

"I'll have to look it up and get back to you," she said.

He called the Tucson Police Department. The detective assigned to the case said, "It was a horrible mess. Two of the nicest kids. They'd just had a big write-up in the paper a couple months before the accident. Best baseball players we ever had around here. Each one a prospect for the majors. Lots of attention from the scouts."

"Anything unusual about the home life?"

"Nice enough kids. One was kind of arrogant about all the attention he got. His folks were pretty well off, but the other kid was from an ordinary middle-class part of town."

Turner asked about the state of the bodies. They knew nothing about genitals being crushed and no one had noticed the absence of underwear.

At 12:05 Fenwick slammed his phone down and gave a shout. "We've got crushed nuts in Odessa, Texas!"

Fenwick and Turner marched up to Blessing's desk on the fourth floor. Fenwick said, "Match every case we've got against ours here, the one in Spokane, Washington, and this one in Odessa, Texas. See if any profiles begin to match. The more matches you get, put them to the top of the pile for follow-up phone calls."

On the way to Aunt Millie's Bar and Grill for lunch, Fenwick gave Turner the details about the Odessa case. "Kid from the local basketball team got stabbed. Found by a custodian at center court of the basketball gym first thing one morning. Sometime during the night the school had been broken into and the kid killed. They still haven't figured out why or how the boy got lured into the school. Coroner recorded one hundred eleven stab wounds. Kid must have looked like a ghastly pincushion."

"Got a profile on the dead boy?"

"Low grades, bad attitude, hell of a basketball player. Been in trouble with school authorities and the police, but could play basketball like a dream."

"Why not just cut off his testicles?" Turner asked.

"Huh?"

"Picture it," Turner said. "The killer is stabbing this guy long after he's dead. Killer must have blood all over himself. But he's also brought along a convenient blunt instrument that he then applies to the kid's balls. Make sense to you? And he's got to carry the knife, blunt whatsis, and get the kid to follow along. How'd he lure him there and did the kid have his underwear?"

"Don't know about the luring part, but the kid did have his underwear on."

"Shit."

"Well, you can't expect a serial killer to be perfect every time."

"I don't like the different methods of killing," Turner said.

"But crushing their nuts has got to be a connection. It's just too obvious."

Fenwick parked the car, turned off the engine, let out a whoosh of breath, and said, "The only thing to do at this point is eat lunch."

SEVEN

At Aunt Millie's they worked their way back to the unofficial Area Ten detective booth. They found Rodriguez staring into a beer. Dwayne and Jennifer were arguing over which was the favorite autopsy they'd attended. All three looked up as Turner and Fenwick plopped down.

"You guys look awful optimistic," Rodriguez said.

"They got a break on the case," Dwayne said. "They're all agog with excitement."

"Remember when we finally got that break on the guy throwing boiling water on prostitutes?" Jennifer asked.

"We toasted with champagne," Dwayne said. "Several of the best vintages."

Turner and Fenwick ordered food and then explained what they'd gotten.

"Great!" Rodriguez said. "Somebody's running around the countryside mowing down teenage delinquents. Fucking fantastic! Fewer gang members on the streets. Less crime. You aren't planning to try and catch this guy?"

"We want to find him so you can pin a medal on him," Fenwick said.

"Using that computer stuff is smart," Dwayne said. "We take at least one computer class a year. We learned a lot more than those FBI people can ever come up with. Be happy to help if you need to understand something."

"We could show you how to streamline your data," Jennifer said. "You sure you need that many categories on all of those cases?"

"Why don't you both sit on it and rotate?" Fenwick suggested.

Dwayne and Jennifer laughed condescendingly.

"Don't be offended," Dwayne said.

"We're just trying to help," Jennifer said.

The waitress delivered Turner and Fenwick's clump of food. Even the presence of Dwayne and Jennifer couldn't sour Turner and Fenwick's upbeat mood.

Back at Area Ten headquarters, several more large cartons of materials had been collected from the library. As Turner opened one box, papers cascaded out. Six more computers had arrived from 11th and State while they were at lunch.

The commander and the chief of detectives stopped by as Turner and Fenwick moved to speak with Blessing. They explained what they'd gotten so far.

The chief of detectives, Samuel Parkingson, was a tall, thin man with a balding head and bushy eyebrows.

"I think it's promising," Parkingson decreed after hearing them out. "I think I should announce it to the media."

"No!" Turner, Fenwick, Blessing, and the commander said simultaneously. Fenwick's faced showed signs of red deepening to purple.

"We need to give the public something," Parkingson said. "The parents of Goldstein and Douglas deserve to know something."

Before Fenwick could blow up, the commander began walking

away with Parkingson. Turner figured their boss feared another outburst at a police brass person. He knew the commander would do everything he could to dissuade Parkingson from committing the incredible blunder of giving their most promising lead to the media.

Fenwick said, "Why the hell do we have PR people in positions where we need competence?"

"Can't all be brilliant detectives like us," Turner said.

Fenwick said, "With this many reporters around and this many cops working, somebody's going to blab about what we're focusing on."

"Probably," Turner said. Nothing they could do about it.

Turner and Fenwick gathered the most promising cases from Blessing and returned to their desks on the third floor to begin making phone calls.

Randy Carruthers bounced up to their desks. "You guys seen Rodriguez lately?" he asked.

"Millie's around an hour ago," Fenwick said.

"I think he's trying to avoid me," Carruthers said.

"We've all been doing that for years," Fenwick muttered.

Carruthers didn't or chose not to hear. Turner thought the fresh-faced creep must hear some of the comments his colleagues made almost daily in front of his face. Either the guy's ego was so huge or his stupidity so massive or his shame so deep that he never showed that he caught on.

"Heard you guys got your big break," Carruthers said.

"We're working on it now," Fenwick said.

Carruthers sat his butt on the edge of Fenwick's desk as if prepared to move in and chat for days.

"Randy, we're awful busy," Turner said.

"Get the fuck out of here," Fenwick said, swiping a massive paw at Carruthers's butt. "Why don't you go find a white Ford Bronco to chase?"

Carruthers jumped off the desk. "I think I'll go hunt up Rodriguez," he said. "We're supposed to be in court this afternoon. He's always late." He trundled away.

132

Around four when the squad room was quiet because of the change of shifts, Turner called Ben and told him he wouldn't be able to go with him to the Bulls game.

"I'm sorry, Ben. I truly am. Like I said, I'll make it up to you."

"I love you," Ben said.

Turner glanced around the squad room. No one but Fenwick was near. He wasn't specifically embarrassed to say what he was going to say next in front of the group because he was gay, but because anybody caught expressing too much affection could get razzed about it. "I love you," he whispered.

Ben said, "I think maybe I just won't go to the game."

"It's courtside seats. Someone will go with you. What about Myra?"

"Her lover's taking her out for her birthday. And she only goes to hockey games."

"You'll find somebody who wants to go."

"I wish it was us," Ben said.

"I do too," Turner said.

"What's Brian doing tonight?" Ben asked.

"You don't have to take my kid," Turner said.

"He and I get along well. Last couple nights were the first times we were around each other much without you there. It would be another chance for him and me to talk about you."

"He doesn't have plans that I know about. I'll check with him, or Rose Talucci will know what he's up to. She's got radar when it comes to monitoring my kids."

"I can ask him," Ben said. "I don't mind."

"He'd like that," Turner said.

Ben agreed, then said, "You know it's around the neighborhood about Rose being sick. Word is she threw a passel of people out of the house around noon today. Told them they were all ghouls and warned them that if they didn't stop whining and moaning, she'd live to be a hundred."

"Good for Rose."

Ben called back half an hour later. Rose would watch Jeff and the ecstatic Brian would go to the game with Ben.

Turner and Fenwick spent hours making phone calls. Not a one gave another clue. They found that many of the people who had been in charge of the cases had moved, transferred, or were simply not in. They got a few simple "I don't knows." Most were sympathetic. Nobody had records of testicles crushed or underwear missing. Those they got hold of gave them more information for the profiles they were building, so after every few calls Turner or Fenwick would take the data upstairs and add it to the stacks of material to be entered on the computer records. At nine, Turner and Fenwick trudged up to the fourth floor together.

Blessing stood at a printer gazing at data running from the machine. Cops bent over data or squinted at screens. The sound of clicking computer keys filled the room.

"Got anything?" Turner asked the computer expert.

"Latest printout coming," Blessing said. "It'll take a few minutes."

Turner gazed at the machine spewing out information. "I thought we had something."

"Easy to get discouraged," Blessing said. "We're still crunching tons of data. You tell them to stop researching at 1950?"

"Yeah," Turner said. "I wanted to give it some kind of cutoff. If we have to do the forties and even the thirties, we will."

"Could a serial killer operate that long without being caught, or at least noticed?" Fenwick asked. "Plus, we go back to the thirties and forties and it means our serial killer is in his seventies or eighties. Seems a little unlikely to me."

"I hope we don't have to go that far back," Blessing said.

Turner wandered over to the floor-to-ceiling corkboard. It was crammed with crime scene photos, copies of lab reports, diagrams, office reports, computer printouts, and the large-scale map. Turner gazed at the multicolored states, a few nearly obliterated by red pins. The entire United States, huge parts of Canada, and much of northern Mexico were filled with red dots. Someone had gone out and brought in a box of a thousand of them. Turner estimated two thirds of the box was empty.

Fenwick joined him at the map. "Not a hell of a lot of help."

134

"Let's get the most likely ones we've been calling all day and use a different color for them," Turner suggested.

They returned a couple minutes later with printouts and began placing yellow pins in the cities they'd been calling.

Fifteen minutes later Fenwick stepped back and said, "I think I see the face of Aunt Millie emerging from the pattern."

"A miracle," Turner said. "We could set up a little shrine and make money off the tourists." He eyed the result critically. "Doesn't have the wart on her cheek the way it should."

Blessing joined them. "Here's the latest." He held the computer printout to show them. "I've rearranged the data. With this kind of spreadsheet, I can print the categories you wanted across the top plus I started five people on going back to the likely cases, taking every piece of data from them and making new categories. Depending on the news stories, you get lots of data or a little. The most I have is one with seventy-three categories, a math genius and track star who fell in a hiking accident back in 1985. All the papers we've been hunting through had him. Data from calls other than the ones you made is still coming in. Also around three this afternoon I had all of the dead teenagers alphabetized by last name. Easier to get duplicate articles about their deaths organized."

Fenwick and Turner nodded. They spread out the data sheets on the three-by-nine-foot table under the map. Blessing had their three testicles-crushed cases at the top of the page. One had thirty categories filled in; another had sixty-three; the third had fifty-one. This reflected the vagaries of the newspaper articles and the information they'd gotten over the phone or by fax.

The next twenty-seven listings were the most likely cases, and the ones they had called. The three men studied the data. Nothing seemed consistent. Some had divorced parents, some hadn't, some had big funerals attended by hundreds, others private affairs, some were accidents, others suicides, some gang problems; only two definitely murders. The accidents had an enormous range: car crashes, fires, falls, hit by lightning—anything humans were prey to happened to these kids.

"I want consistency," Fenwick said.

"Forget it," Blessing said. "The only reason some of these came to the top was their sort of relation in a few categories to your three. The kids played sports, but that's the only connection."

The cops shook their heads.

"Shame about a few of these kids," Blessing said.

"Why's that?" Turner asked.

Blessing pointed to a column far on the right of the lengthy printout. "Five of these had big spreads in their local papers sometime in the year before they died."

Turner could neither move nor talk.

"Goldstein and Douglas had articles about them, too," Fenwick said.

"Brian did last month," Turner said.

"That's the connection?" Blessing asked.

"So few have it," Fenwick said.

Turner rushed to a computer with the others hurrying behind. "Make this give me data," Turner said. "I want kids who died who had articles written about them."

"We don't have that many local papers," Blessing said as his fingers raced over the keys. "In our 'most likely' category, only those five mentioned it. I'm not sure about all these others. We only know about it if one of the national papers picked it up."

"Make the damn thing give data!" Turner commanded.

Fenwick put his hand on Turner's shoulder. "Easy, buddy."

Minutes passed as Blessing typed, watched the screen, and typed some more.

Turner sent one of the cops to find out if the Bulls game was over. It wasn't.

Finally the printer began to click.

"We've only got two more besides these," Blessing said.

"Where are they?" Turner asked.

"Huh?" Blessing said.

Turner snatched the page out of Blessing's hand. He hurried to the map, found seven blue pins, and jammed them into the map.

"They start in Spokane and make a circle through the Southwest to St. Louis," Turner said.

Fenwick had been staring at the printout. "Look at the dates. Started nine years ago, but they're in order. Spokane was first, then Portland. Jesus Christ!"

"My kid's in danger. I've got to get to the stadium!" Turner was already running for the stairs as he spoke.

"I'll go with." Fenwick was right behind.

"I'll call ahead," Blessing yelled. "Do you know where their seats are?"

"Courtside. Behind the Bulls bench," Turner shouted from the top of the stairs.

"Security's tight in that area anyway," Fenwick said as they raced down to the first floor.

Turner jumped in his car and Fenwick threw himself into the passenger side as Turner floored the engine. Fenwick's driving was as nothing compared to the speed Turner made to the stadium.

They showed their badges at the gate, whose keeper was inclined to give them a hard time. Turner barged past, found a security guard, showed him his identification and dragged the mystified man in his wake. He didn't care if the guy understood any of the explanation Turner shouted at him as they ran toward the seats. He was going to get to his son. At the entrance way to the mass of humanity, a contingent of security guards met them.

"You the cops we got the call about—looking for somebody?"

"Yes," Turner said.

"We haven't been able to find them," the security guard said. "The guy who called couldn't give us much of a description."

"They're here," Turner said. He and Fenwick, followed by two of the stadium security guards, marched down to the section behind the Bulls bench.

They found two empty seats. The nearby fans resented the intrusion. No one could remember who was in the seats, and no one remembered anyone being in them since halftime.

The head of security at the United Center joined them after a few minutes. "Who are you looking for?" he asked.

"My son, Brian, a teenager, and a guy he was here with in his late thirties."

No one had seen them. They were not in the first-aid station. An all-building page turned up nothing. Turner, Fenwick, and the head of security stood in the main foyer of the building. A commotion broke out at the gate twenty feet from them.

"Ben," Paul called as he ran toward his lover.

Ben had blood on his face and hands.

"What happened? Where's Brian?"

"In the car. Unconscious. I couldn't get in. He wanted to drive. Took his car. He's got the keys."

"Where?"

Ben staggered out the door. He pointed toward the west parking lot. "Row six or seven across the street."

Paul ran across the well-lit parking lot. He thought he heard people behind him. He nearly tripped on the curb on the far side of the street. His eyes desperately scanned the thousands of cars for his son's. He turned down row six and slowed slightly. A security guard ran up next to him.

"You see the car?" the guard asked.

Paul shook his head. He ran a few more steps. "There," he shouted. He raced toward his son's car. It was parked at an odd angle. His son was sprawled in the back seat. Brian didn't move.

Paul pulled out his keys, unlocked the front door, flipped the switch to unlock all the doors, wrenched open the back door, and grabbed his son. He felt the strong pulse at the throat. He was alive, but tears came anyway.

Brian had nasty scrapes on the left side of his face and on both hands. Paul held him and tried to revive him, but had no luck. Paramedics arrived quickly. Brian revived after a few seconds of oxygen. He lay on the gurney holding his dad's hand and looking bewildered.

Paul let the paramedics work but stayed next to his son. After a few minutes Brian sat up. He held his head with both hands and bent over.

"Are you okay?" Paul asked.

"My head feels like shit, but I think I'm all right."

One paramedic said, "He might have a concussion. You should probably take him to a hospital."

"What happened?" Paul asked.

"A security guard gave me a message from you."

"I sent no message."

"He said you wanted me to meet you out front. I said I'd go get Ben, but the guard said it was urgent and he'd tell him, and we could meet out front."

Fenwick, hovering nearby, said, "I'll go talk to security." He hurried off.

Brian continued, "I got outside, but nobody was here. I thought of going back in, but I figured maybe you'd pull up in an unmarked car, so I walked toward the street."

Brian took a deep breath. "When I got to the curb, a car pulled out of the far end of the parking lot and started driving down the street. He was going pretty fast, but I didn't think anything of it until he swerved toward me. I leaped sideways as the car jumped the curb. It was a little higher than whoever it was thought, because the car thumped and swerved sideways, or he'd have hit me. Then he backed off and tried to hit me again. I was running by that time. I headed into the middle of the cars, away from the street. I didn't run back to the building because there was nothing but open space between me and it. Guy would have had a clear shot at me.

"I dodged between cars. He tried ramming a few. I jumped up on the hood of one. He was smart. He smashed into the one I was jumping toward. He moved it enough that I mistimed my leap. I fell between the cars and bashed my head. I was really groggy. I thought if I could get to our car, I could drive away. Nobody was around. Everybody was inside for the game. I ran across the street while he was trying to get out of that part of the parking lot.

139

I was having trouble focusing for a while. He almost got me on this side of the street. It was like dodge-'em cars at a carnival. I don't know how I got in the back seat. I remember getting inside and locking all the doors. He backed up and came at the car as hard as he could. I must have hit my head again. I don't know why he didn't get out of his car and come after me."

Several blue and white Chicago police cars had shown up by now, along with the head of security, as well as a small crowd.

Paul stood next to his son. Ben, who'd been quietly standing on the other side of Brian, said, "I can fill that in a little. When Brian didn't come back from the john for a long time, I got uneasy. I went to look for him. Through the doors I saw Brian run across the street."

The head of security said, "My people saw something wrong. Thought it was a couple of teenagers screwing around. They weren't fast enough to get out here to help. When they heard cars getting smashed, they moved pretty quick."

"I got there first," Ben said. "As I got near Brian's car, this guy pulled out and tried to hit me. I fell and banged my head against the pavement and scraped my hands like Brian."

Fenwick walked up. He said, "They're checking again, but no message came through security central for Brian."

"It was the killer," Turner said. "What did the guy look like who gave you the message?"

"Shorter than me. Chubby. A guard-type uniform." Brian looked at one of the nearby guards. "Didn't look like his."

"Probably fake," Fenwick said.

Brian continued, "Official-looking hat on his head. Long black hair. Big bushy mustache. Glasses."

"I didn't get a look at him behind the headlights," Ben said.

"What kind of car was it?" Turner asked.

Fenwick interrupted, "We got a report of an abandoned wreck a block and a half from here. I talked to one of the cops. No license plates. No current registration. We'll impound. Try for fingerprints."

Paul insisted on a stop at the hospital for Brian and Ben,

140

although both said it wasn't necessary. In a mercifully brief time, they confirmed that Brian's concussion was very minor, but that he should take it easy for a few days.

At home Paul examined every room in the house carefully before allowing anyone inside. He hurried over to Mrs. Talucci's to retrieve Jeff. He told her the news and ran back.

Fenwick said, "I've got uniformed cops on the way."

"Is there going to be shooting, Dad?" Jeff asked.

"No, son. We're just being careful."

Ben stood quietly in the background.

Brian said, "Jose was in the article, too."

"We've got to warn them," Paul said.

"I can do that," Brian said.

"No. It should be somebody from the police. We'll stop before we go back to the station. We've got to follow this lead. The boys will be safe here after protection arrives."

"I can stay the night," Ben offered.

"Thanks," Paul said. "Even with cops nearby, I'd prefer to have somebody they know around. We can stop at Jose Martin's on our way back."

"I want to go with you," Brian said.

"It's not necessary."

"You've never met Jose's dad," Brian said. "I can help talk to him with you. I'd like to be there when you tell Jose. He's my friend. If we're in danger. . . ."

"We should send uniforms to cover their house until we get there," Fenwick said.

"I want you here, son," Paul said. "We'd have to make a trip back just to drop you off."

"Dad, I really think I should be there."

"Why?"

"Well, because. . . ." Brian hesitated.

"It'll be fine," Paul said.

"Dad. . . ." Brian began another protest, but shrugged his shoulders and stopped abruptly. He looked confused and upset. Paul could see his son wanted to make more objections. He

141

couldn't figure out what the big deal was about Brian wanting to go.

"It's nearly midnight," Fenwick said. "Should we call ahead?"

"They go to bed early," Brian said.

"If we're going to wake them out of a sound sleep, we should be there to explain it and not try talking over the phone and then showing up. Let's just go."

Uniformed cops in a squad car took up their post outside the house. Brian gave his dad Jose's address. After assuring Jeff he would not be able to see gunfire if he stayed awake, they left.

They found the tiny bungalow on Hubbard Street two blocks east of Western Avenue. A postmidnight hush enveloped the well-lit, tree-lined street. They found two cops sitting in a squad car at the curb.

"Anything?" Turner asked them after introductions were over.

"Couldn't be quieter. What's going on?"

"Connected to the Goldstein murder," Fenwick said.

"Wow," one of the uniforms said. "Anything we can do?"

"We'll try and set up people to watch here all night. Tomorrow we'll figure out a better situation."

They turned from the car and walked up the cement walk. The well-trimmed grass was still green from the recent rains and unseasonable warmth. Turner and Fenwick wore only sport coats in the mid-sixties weather.

The embankment for the Northwestern Train tracks loomed behind the house. No lights were on inside. Turner rang the bell and banged on the front door several times before he saw lights turn on through a curtained window on their left. For a minute he thought maybe they should have called ahead.

The porch light flicked on and a voice called through the door, "Who is it?"

"Paul Turner, Brian Turner's dad. I'm a police officer. It's important, Mr. Martin. We have to talk to you."

The door opened several inches. Realizing he'd never met Mr.

Martin, Turner pulled out his identification and held it up. No lights shone in the space immediately behind the man, and the outside bulb only illuminated the bottom half of the doorway. Turner couldn't get a good look at Martin's face.

"What's this about?" Mr. Martin asked. He made no move to open the door any further.

"We think Jose is in danger," Turner said. "We'd like to explain what's wrong."

"He's here. He's not in danger."

"What is it, Will?" Turner recognized Jose's voice from deeper in the house. He didn't know any kids who called their parents by their first names, but he ignored the slightly jarring note. He didn't care about their family relationships. He just wanted to warn them and get back to Area Ten headquarters.

He saw the face he could barely make out turn away. He heard Mr. Martin's muffled voice, "Police. I might have to let them in. Go put some clothes on." The face turned back to them.

"We've got a squad out here all ready, and we've got back-up protection coming," Turner said.

"We haven't done anything wrong," Mr. Martin said.

"I know you haven't. We have reason to believe your son is in danger. Can we come in?" A timely warning was turning into a hassle. He wondered why.

Lights flicked on in the living room and the door slowly eased open. The room they entered was painted white. A thirty-five-inch-screen television sat in one corner. Individual pieces of a complete set of brown leather-covered living-room furniture were backed against three walls: a couch, love seat, and two reclining chairs. The rug was off-white and spotless. One wall was devoted to sports trophies on rows of bookshelves. Another had a twenty-by-thirty-inch painting of an autumn scene in a mountain valley. A third had a poster of an athletic-looking man's bare chest and jean-clad hips. He was holding a baby against his chest—a young father with a newborn. On top of the television was an eighteen-by-twenty-four-inch black and white picture of

Mr. Martin and his son, their faces close together and smiling. They had their arms around each other's shoulders. Behind them was a crowd in front of a float from a parade.

Turner and Fenwick sat on the chairs. Mr. Martin sat on the couch. He wore gray knit pants and a plain white T-shirt. He hadn't put on shoes or socks. His bushy, inch-thick mustache seemed an odd contrast to the burr-cut hair on his head. On his upper arm he had a tattoo that was half covered by the T-shirt. Turner couldn't make out what it was.

Wearing jeans, white socks, and a baggy sweatshirt, Jose entered the room and sat next to his dad. He greeted Turner courteously.

Turner immediately noticed that while Jose's skin was dusty gold, his dad's was bright pink. The father's frame was bulky but not fat, and gave no hint of the lean strength of the son. Turner wondered about the difference, but both father and son were looking at him with puzzled expressions waiting for an explanation of this late night intrusion. Turner noted that Mr. Martin's right hand held the left rigidly. He did not wear a wedding ring.

Turner explained about the case and the possibility of there being danger for Jose.

"We don't want trouble," Mr. Martin said when he finished.

"We think we should leave some uniformed officers outside for tonight and then they can set up a detail at the school tomorrow," Turner said. "We can figure out what to do on a more regular basis after that."

"How long is this going to last?" Martin asked.

"As long as it takes to catch the killer," Fenwick said.

"We don't want to bother the police," Martin said.

"It's not a bother and the danger is real," Turner said.

"I don't know," Martin said. "Didn't sound like you really had a lot of information to go on. Aren't you overreacting a little bit?"

Martin's voice was gruff and unyielding. Turner wondered what the problem was.

"Not if there's a possibility my son is in danger," Turner said.

"Will . . . , Dad," Jose said. "It'll be okay. They'll catch the guy and everything will be fine."

Martin looked doubtful. "I can protect my kid myself."

"Eventually you'll have to go to work," Fenwick said.

"The cops can't protect him forever either," Martin countered. "You'll be lucky to get much support now. You can't stay for days, weeks, and months."

"We can get protection for the immediate problem," Turner said. "We might be able to get some of the task force people freed up. The only permanent solution is catching the killer. Until then, we'll think of something."

"I don't know," Martin said.

"Dad," Jose said. "It'll be fine."

"The cops won't need to come in the house?" Martin asked.

"No," Turner said.

"Okay, I guess."

A few minutes of discussion of logistics followed, then the detectives left.

"That was odd," Fenwick said in the car.

"You mean odd-funny or odd-illegal?"

"I'm not sure. Something didn't sit right."

"It was strange all right, although, think about it. You get woken up out of a sound sleep and given the news that your kid is in danger, it can throw you," Turner said.

"I suppose they aren't the first father and son not to look much alike," Fenwick said.

"Didn't look alike at all," Turner said.

"Maybe he's adopted."

"Possible."

"And where's the mother?"

"I'll have to ask Brian. I don't know these people. I kind of like Jose, but I'm sure I've never seen his dad at any of their games. That burr-cut head is noticeable on top of that bushy mustache."

"I don't like kids who call their parents by their first names," Fenwick said. "Always sounds wrong to me when I hear it. I guess

I'm old-fashioned. The tattoo was closer to you. What was it?"

"Couldn't tell. You know that picture on the television was odd, too. Not sure why."

"Odd how?"

"I don't know. I've got to think about it."

"They probably took a photo and had it blown up," Fenwick said.

"Yeah, but there was something about it." Turner shrugged.

By 1:00 A.M. they were on the fourth floor of Area Ten headquarters with half the crew from the task force still working. They pored over cases involving fatal accidents, suicides, or murders that had any connection to kids who played sports and had had articles written about them. It was late now for getting much information, but they could talk to police departments in the larger cities. Coroners and medical examiners would have to wait until the morning.

"We got the background on that football player, Waverly?" Fenwick asked Blessing.

"Yeah. He was in Seattle in 1985 in college when the killing in Spokane occurred."

"Close enough," Fenwick said.

"And in 1991 for the Odessa, Texas, killing he was trying to make it onto a pro team practicing in New England somewhere."

"Not close," Turner said.

"I want more information on him," Fenwick said. "Anything you can find."

Around two, Fenwick asked, "Are we going to start calling the families of these more likely cases?"

"I'm not sure for what," Turner said.

"More data? Facts missing from these reports. If these were murders and not accidents, they were never asked all the questions we need answered."

"I'm not sure I'd want to open up some of these old wounds over the phone. We wouldn't be able to prove we're cops. I'd rather do it in person with valid identification and maybe a local cop or two to smooth the way."

"We aren't going to be able to travel around the country on the strength of the evidence we've got so far."

"We better wait on calls to the families," Turner said. "If it becomes necessary, we can do it. When we call the local papers today, we should get more information."

"Better make sure the callers know what questions to ask."

"Yeah, I've got a list of instructions for what I want them to find out."

Blessing came over to them. "I've got to get some sleep," he said.

"We've got another box of articles to go through from the library," Turner said. "We're going to stick with it. I want to start making calls as soon as we can in the morning. We've been concentrating west of the Mississippi because of what we've got so far."

"You've got some in the East," Blessing said.

"Not as many," Fenwick said.

Blessing shook his head. "I gotta sleep. I'll be back by ten."

Turner and Fenwick pored over the copies of articles in the last box for another hour.

"This better be all of it," Fenwick said.

"Should be. We've got the accident, suicide, or murder reports on every kid that an article appeared on in seven major papers since 1985. I hope by noon we can have all of the data on the computers and we'll have new stuff from more phone calls."

"If we're lucky."

"Yeah. Brian's in danger and I'm going to solve this."

"We'll work it out," Fenwick assured him.

Too exhausted to keep their eyes open, they left a little after three. Paul crawled into bed next to Ben and immediately dropped off to sleep.

He awoke at seven. After a shower, he arrived downstairs to find Ben fixing bacon and eggs at the stove, and Jeff with his nose in a book at the kitchen table. He heard Brian's footsteps upstairs hurrying from bathroom to bedroom as he finished dressing.

"You ever going to get some sleep, Dad?" Jeff asked.

"I got a few hours last night. Maybe later this week, I hope." Paul hugged Jeff and then Ben.

Brian thudded downstairs and hurried into the kitchen. "What's going on, Dad?" he asked. "What happened at Jose's?" He pulled a pineapple and a cantaloupe out of the refrigerator. He grabbed a knife from the dish drainer in the sink, sat at the kitchen table, and began cutting into the fruit. Paul took some newspapers off the chair near the back door and put them under where Brian was cutting.

"You feeling okay?" Paul asked.

"I'm fine. A little sore, maybe. It's nothing."

Paul told Brian about meeting Jose and his dad.

"So everything went okay?" Brian asked after Paul finished.

"Yeah, shouldn't it have?" Paul asked.

"Sure," Brian said. "Is it okay for Jose to come over and study tonight? We've got a big final on *Great Expectations* tomorrow. We want to go over our notes."

"You actually read the book?"

"Both of us did. Jose really liked it. He says he's going to be an English major in college."

"Good for him. Yeah, he can come over and study," Paul said. "We've got security for both of you set. You've met Jose's dad, right?"

"Yeah."

Brian managed to imbue this monosyllable with more teenage annoyance than Paul had heard from his son in two years.

"Is there a problem?" Paul asked.

"No."

Extremely wary and as alert as he could be on less than four hours' sleep, Paul asked questions carefully. "His dad struck me as kind of gruff and unpleasant," he said.

"I don't think he likes people. The guys don't go to Jose's

house much. I've only been a few times. Mostly we stay in the rec room in the basement. We try not to bother his dad."

"Jose seemed to like him."

"They get along great."

"Jose calls his dad by his first name?"

"I guess he does."

"Either you know or you don't," Paul said.

"Yeah, I've heard him call his dad by his first name. Why are you questioning me?"

"You're handier than Jose or his dad. Am I missing something? All my cop instincts tell me something's not right here. Are you hiding something?"

"I'm not lying about anything."

"Not lying is one thing. Holding back information is another. What's wrong between Jose and his dad?"

"Nothing. They get along fine."

"I didn't see his mother last night."

"Oh."

"Not 'oh.' Do you know anything about his mother?"

"She hasn't been around for years. Jose never sees her."

"Jose doesn't look much like his dad. Do you know if he's adopted?"

"He's not adopted."

Paul tried to catch his son's gaze, but Brian concentrated on peeling and chopping and not looking directly at his dad.

"I've never noticed Mr. Martin at a game," Paul said.

"Maybe he's shy or he doesn't like football?"

"When his son is the star quarterback and had his picture on the front page of the sports section of the *Chicago Tribune,* you'd think he'd crow about it. I did."

"I don't know why he acts the way he does. Maybe you should ask him."

"Maybe I will."

Heavy amounts of teenage exasperation had been creeping into Brian's tone. "I don't know what's going on, okay? I don't know anything about the two of them or. . . ." Brian stopped."

149

"The two of them or what?"

Brian finished slicing the pineapple and cantaloupe, threw out the dregs, took out dishes, and placed servings for four on the table. Ben silently served the eggs and bacon. The four of them began to eat.

"The two of them or what?" Paul reiterated.

Brian shrugged his broad shoulders and twisted his head as far as he could left and right. He stood up, got himself a glass, opened the refrigerator, and poured himself cold bottled water. He guzzled it for several seconds.

"Look, Brian," Paul said. "You guys are in danger and I need to know as much as possible. Even the smallest thing could be important. A dangerous killer could be after you."

"It has nothing to do with the killings or any danger."

"So there is something."

Brian sat back down. "I hate when you question me like you're a cop."

"You only hate it when you've done something wrong. Have you done something wrong?"

"No. And neither has Jose or his dad."

"Then why won't you tell me about it?"

"You wouldn't understand."

Paul stopped himself from slamming his fork down on the table. Paul and Brian were closer than most fathers and sons. Paul had always attributed it to that fact that he'd told Brian about his sexual orientation when the boy was eight years old. He didn't think Brian understood it completely then, but he was glad he had told him at that age. Early on he'd been able to resolve questions and confusions about a father who was different. Plus he'd always tried reason with his sons rather than angry commands for resolving difficulties. Paul was exhausted from the lack of sleep and the long days he'd been putting in. He didn't know if he had the patience left to dredge up a reasonable response to his son's comment. He shut his eyes, rubbed his fingers against his eyelids, then placed his hands flat on the table top and looked at Brian, whose fists were clenched. Brian shook his head back and forth and refused to raise his eyes to meet his father's.

Ben reached across the table and placed his hand gently on Paul's forearm. Paul glanced at the concern in his lover's eyes. He drew a deep breath.

Paul said, "I've always been honest with you, Brian. You've always been honest with me. When haven't I tried to understand? You know I always listen. It really hurts that you would say that to me. That really bothers me. Do you actually think there is something you would tell me that I wouldn't try to understand?"

"Do you want me to leave?" Ben asked.

Without removing his gaze from Brian's downturned face, Paul said softly, "It's all right. Please stay."

Jeff stared at the adults and his older brother. Paul saw moisture gathering in his eyes. Paul couldn't remember this kind of all-out fight with his teenage son.

Jeff whispered, "Please don't fight."

Paul placed a hand on his younger son's arm. "Everything's going to be all right," he murmured. He looked at Brian, who was staring at his younger brother.

Brian hung his head for a minute. He didn't look up as he began to speak. "I'm sorry, Dad. I didn't mean. . . . It's just you're a cop and. . . . Ah, nuts!" Brian picked up his fork and began fiddling with it. "I'm really sorry about what I said. I know I can trust you more than any guy I know can trust his dad. I was frustrated." Brian finally raised his eyes and looked at his dad. "I'm really sorry, honest."

Paul put his arm on Brian's shoulder and squeezed gently. "It's okay," he said. "I'm real tired. Maybe I'm pushing too hard, but I'm concerned about you."

"I understand," Brian said.

"They aren't doing something illegal, like drugs?"

"No, Dad. None of the guys I hang out with would do that stuff. One of the guys at the party. . . . I made one of them leave because he brought drugs."

"Good." Paul didn't mention he'd guessed as much.

"You don't want to know who?"

"If you want to tell me, and it's important."

"No. It's okay."

Paul said, "We're losing the main topic here, which is Jose and his dad."

Brian set the fork down. "I promised I'd never tell. It doesn't have anything to do with any killing. You just said that if it was important about the kid at the party, it was my choice on telling you. If we're going to trust each other, it's got to be about things we do tell and the stuff we don't."

Paul held his elder son's gaze. "I have a killer to catch. I have you to protect. You're asking me to accept your judgment."

"You have in the past."

"I don't know if anything has been as dangerous as this."

"Depends on how much of an adult you think I am. You've talked to me like an equal for a long time. I like our relationship, especially when I see a lot of the other guys having fights with their parents. I don't ever want to fight with you. I don't want to keep secrets from you. This is not my secret to tell. Dad, ask Jose, or Mr. Martin, okay? Say the things you've said to me to them. Honest, Dad, the secret can't have anything to do with the murders, but ask Jose, ask Mr. Martin. Please, Dad, not me."

If the secret did have something to do with the killing and Paul missed it because he trusted his boy, he'd have to justify that to his conscience for a long time, especially if any harm came of it to his own son.

"He'll be here tonight. You can ask him then."

Paul agreed reluctantly.

"You going to warn him I'm going to talk to him tonight?" Paul asked.

"Not if you don't want me to."

"Don't," Paul said. "Please."

His son agreed.

E   I   G   H   T

Turner drove back to Area Ten headquarters through a cool swirling breeze which held the first puffs of winter. He found Fenwick examining the crime scene photos on the corkboard on the fourth floor. Fenwick had on a clean shirt and was freshly shaved.

"Anything new?" Turner asked.

"I'm more tired than ever," Fenwick said. He handed Turner some forms.

"What's this?"

"Previous owners of all the buildings in a three-block radius of the warehouse. No names of anybody we questioned so far. Couple of corporations I've got uniforms checking out."

Turner picked up a manila envelope from a stack of twenty. He opened it. "What's this?" he asked.

"Pictures of Waverly and a select group of nobodies to bring around to everybody we talked to."

It was more efficient than lineups to bring groups of photos around to witnesses for possible identification. Real lineups would follow positive responses from any witnesses. This would be a preliminary stage. Turner and Fenwick plus other members of the task force would show them around today.

The commander appeared at the top of the stairs and hurried over to them. He spoke without preamble. "You ever hear of a Peter Volmer, all-state soccer star the past two years? Got scholarships to half a dozen universities?"

"Don't follow soccer much," Turner said.

Poindexter said, "They did a big spread on him in the *Tribune* a month ago."

"He's dead," Fenwick said.

"Call came in a few minutes ago from Millwood, a village in Kane County. If your theory is right, we've got another one. We better think about notifying every kid who's had his name in the paper in the metropolitan area."

"As soon as possible," Turner said.

"I'll work on it while you're gone," Poindexter said.

"They expecting us in Millwood?" Fenwick asked.

Poindexter nodded.

In the old part of Millwood they found a rambling Victorian mansion surrounded by a plethora of emergency vehicles. They identified themselves to the cops outside, then entered onto gleaming hardwood floors and the sounds of incredible shrieking.

Their contact was Detective Smithers. He was about five feet five and slender. He wore a brown suit the same color as his mustache. Introductions over, he beckoned them into an alcove to the right of the front door.

Smithers shook his head. "Hear that?"

Turner and Fenwick nodded.

"The mother. Got home fifteen minutes ago. She and the husband had a breakfast political meeting. Left this morning at six. Their kid was alive."

"What happened?"

"Worst I've ever seen." He led them to a set of double doors and pushed them further open.

If it had been their first homicide, Turner and Fenwick would have gasped and one or both would have run to the washroom to lose their breakfast.

From a chandelier in the middle of a two-story foyer/living room hung a naked body. Thick ribbons of flesh and muscle hung from great gashes in the torso and every limb. Some of the cuts had gone deep enough and several of the gouges were sufficiently wide to reveal bones and organs inside. An enormous pool of blood covered a white and purple Persian rug. In the middle of the blood was a pair of briefs completely soaked in blood.

Smithers turned away.

Fenwick muttered in Turner's ear, "Let's have another one, just like the other one."

Turner barely kept his composure.

Smithers said, "My boss will be here soon. I've never handled anything like this."

Since this was Kane County, the people who examined the crime scene were unfamiliar to Turner and Fenwick. After the Chicago detectives were introduced, and explanations given for their presence, Turner and Fenwick described what they had found so far.

"You really think that's the solution?" a tanned male in his early thirties asked.

"Best we've got," Fenwick said. "What do you have?"

"We're just starting."

"What happened to him?" Fenwick asked.

"Didn't die from being hung. That just kept him in place while the killer worked. Only blood in the house is on the rug here. I think it was the cut that sliced his back nearly in half that actually killed him. Won't know for sure until I get him to the lab. Tape around ankles and wrists kept him immobile."

"Who called it in?" Turner asked.

"Friend who was supposed to pick him up for school walked in."

"He had a key?"

"Don't lock up much out here."

"So that's how the killer got in."

"No forced entry evident."

"Any struggle in the house?"

"His bedroom's a mess."

"What'd the parents say?"

"Mom hasn't stopped shrieking. Dad keeps mumbling, 'We were so happy.' Have to wait a while on them."

"She's running for Congress from this district," Smithers said.

"Anything on the friend who found him?"

"In total shock. Can barely talk. They were best friends since kindergarten."

"What about the dead boy? Good kid? Creep?"

"I knew him," Smithers said. "I coached him on his little league team years ago. Nicest, most polite kid you'd ever want to meet. Town made a big thing out of it when he got the big write-up in the *Tribune.*"

"Killer here used several different knives. Cuts are different sizes. No hacking or sawing. Really sharp knives. From the angle I'd say killer was probably right-handed."

"Neighbors see anything?"

"Canvass of the immediate neighbors is done. We have to get back to the ones who weren't home. So far only one person saw anything unusual. Pickup truck in the driveway about six-thirty. Didn't see anybody. Might have been new. Was not a dark color."

Turner told them about the three different descriptions they'd gotten so far on vehicles.

"At least it was a truck," Fenwick said. "Closest we've had to a match so far."

They asked them to check to see if the boy's testicles were crushed.

As he drove back to Chicago, Fenwick asked, "Is this our killer?"

"I hate the goddamn MOs being different."

"We may have a very, very smart serial killer. Maybe he read all the books that are out about organized and disorganized killers and patterns of behavior."

"It'd have to be three in this area in less than a week. Why kill one in random cities over a number of years and then increase it here?"

"We don't know how many he's killed here or anywhere else."

"He's gone crazier? That's part of the profile. They do more and more. Isn't it supposed to be the more they do, the more they want to get caught?"

"Think so," Fenwick said.

"That could have been my boy," Turner said. "Maybe the killer got frustrated because of his failure last night and this is the result. My boy is alive and this kid is dead."

"Only thing we can do is focus on catching the guy before he tries again."

"Or before he flees the area. Anything here help us catch our guy?"

"Says he might still be in the area."

"We better contact the media damn quick."

"There'll be plenty of them around the station. Better see what the Commander's come up with first."

Before returning to the station, they made three stops to show their photo lineup. The fast-food worker at McDonald's said flat out no, none of them was the guy. At the school of the kid who had found the body, each boy frowned seriously. Two picked out cops who'd been on duty that night.

Last, they stopped at the new fitness center down from where they found Jake Goldstein's body.

Drew Riley let them in.

"Thought you might be working on the north side today," Turner said.

"My day off. Just finished fixing up a room in the back where I can live. I shower and shave at the health club."

He looked carefully at all the photos. "Nobody I recognize. Is one of them the killer?"

"We don't know," Fenwick said. "Could any of them be the person you saw in the car that night?"

Riley hesitated over Waverly's photo.

The cops waited patiently.

Finally Riley shook his head. "No, none of these."

"You hesitated on one of them," Fenwick said.

"I don't want to say unless I'm absolutely certain."

It was no good to press him. You don't put a witness on the stand who isn't absolutely certain, but Turner and Fenwick's level of suspicion about Waverly rose another notch.

The media frenzy outside Area Ten headquarters was incredible. The sea of reporters swamped their car as they came to a halt.

"Why couldn't we have an early season ten-inch snowfall?" Fenwick asked. "That would get their butts out of here, or I could put the car in reverse and there would be lots of new openings in journalism for hardworking college kids."

Suddenly Fenwick rammed open his car door. People jumped back and a ripple effect opened a small path for a few seconds. Turner shoved open his door.

They heard, "Is this new killing connected? What are the police going to do? Are all the departments cooperating? Why wasn't this killing prevented? Is the mayor going to intervene?"

Side by side, slowly, carefully, and silently, Turner and Fenwick made their way into the station.

The commander met them on the first floor. "We're having another press conference."

"I'll never keep my temper," Fenwick said.

"You're not going to be here." The commander motioned them over to a corner away from the admitting desk. "You're going to Kenitkamette. One of the high school kids, Arnie Pantera, is confessing."

"The Satanism kid," Turner said.

"Who?" the commander asked.

Turner got halfway through the explanation of their interview with Arnie before the commander said, "Yeah, now I remember. Get up there. The Kenitkamette police are holding him and are not releasing anything to the press."

"They don't believe him?"

"Get your butts up there and find out what's going on. I've got a goddamn press conference in ten minutes. I didn't think this could get worse."

They waited five minutes for the reporters to begin filing into the building for the press conference before they both hurried out a back way to their car.

"I'd rather stay and follow our leads around the country," Turner said.

"And when you're Commander you too can do whatever you please."

"I'm not sure I want to be Commander."

"I want to be emperor or maybe god of the detectives. Christ, I'm tired. And I'm hungry."

"I just want to sleep."

Just before the border to Kenitkamette they stopped at a Dunkin Donuts for coffee and sustenance. "It's after two already," Fenwick said. "All this driving around is futile."

Chief Robsart ushered them into her office. "This is unreal. Parents are here demanding a lawyer for their kid. Kid is here insisting he doesn't want a lawyer."

"Does he know about the murder in Millwood this morning?" Turner asked.

"Yep. Says he did that one, too."

Turner said, "I want to talk to him with his lawyer present, plus a state's attorney, and his parents."

"You really want everybody there?" Robsart asked.

"Yeah. I don't want any legal or constitutional or procedural or any other kind of technical difficulties. If this kid did it, I want everybody around. What happened?"

"Kid walked in here about eleven. He confessed to the first three people he saw. One was a homeless person we were shipping to County Jail, another was a temporary secretary doing filing for the day, and the last was an officer who's only been working here for two weeks. She had the sense to call me. He tried confessing to me, but after the first sentence, I stopped him. I called the state's attorney, the parents, and you. He's been sitting in a conference room. I think I should have called a team of psychiatrists."

"Arnie is not on the same planet as the rest of us," Turner said.

"You got that right. He's hearing voices the rest of us don't."

Half an hour later, Turner and Fenwick sat in a room that looked out over a dry and empty fountain. Assembled around an oak conference table were all the people that Turner had suggested be present along with Robsart. Two uniformed Kenitkamette cops brought in Arnie Pantera.

Again, he was dressed all in black, including his cape. He gazed slowly at everyone in the room.

The police and the lawyers had agreed that Turner would be the spokesperson for the group.

"Why are all these people here?" Arnie whispered.

Turner said, "We need to talk to you about the killings. These are the people we wanted present."

Arnie took a chair next to Turner.

"The police here said you have a statement to make," Turner said.

Arnie looked around the room again. "Yes," he said. "Yes, the great Satan has spoken to me. I have done his bidding and I am here to tell you about it."

"Did you kill Jake Goldstein, Frank Douglas, and Peter Volmer?"

"Yes." Arnie's voice never rose above a whisper. He didn't look at anyone in the room as he spoke, but stared out at the swirling leaves driven by the cool wind.

"Why did you do it, Arnie?"

"Satan commanded it."

160

"This is ridiculous," Mr. Pantera said. He turned to their lawyer. "I demand you put a stop to this."

The lawyer was an elderly gentleman with a narrow face, bushy eyebrows, and a goatee. He said, "I have informed Arnie of his rights. You were there. I say again, Arnie, I advise you not to speak to the police. This interview should stop immediately."

Turner didn't say a word. He wasn't convinced this kid had done anything yet.

Arnie said, "I wish to tell the world. I have nothing to fear."

Turner wasn't sure he'd get sane answers to any of his questions.

"You may continue asking," Arnie said.

Turner looked at the lawyer and the parents.

"Arnie, listen to me," his father said. "This is insane. You can't do this. You've taken this far enough. You have to stop now."

His mother said, "Arnie, we'll get you all the help we can, but you are only endangering yourself the more you talk."

They spent half an hour debating with Arnie, alternately cajoling and threatening. The cops and state's attorney said little, the lawyer only some, and Arnie least of all.

They took a break, and out in the hall, Turner got hold of the lawyer, Mr. and Mrs. Pantera, and the state's attorney. "Look," he said, "I don't think your kid killed anybody. If you'd let me ask him some specific details about the killings, especially today's murder, I think we can eliminate him as a suspect."

"It's a trick," Mr. Pantera said. "I know how you police trick people."

The lawyer led the parents down the hall out of earshot of Turner. They returned a few minutes later. The lawyer said, "We want to know before we go in what you're going to ask."

Normally Turner would bristle at this, and he saw Fenwick draw a deep breath for a vociferous protest, but Turner said, "Sure. I'm going to ask him about details that didn't happen and see if he confirms them. If he passes that test, I'll ask a few details that he couldn't know that we haven't released to the public. If he confirms them, he did do it."

The lawyer and the parents conferred for another few minutes.

Fenwick said, "Why the hell did you give them that?"

"Do you think he did it?"

"No."

"So we do it their way and we get the hell out of here some-time this century."

Fenwick shrugged.

Everyone reassembled in the room. Turner again sat next to Arnie.

"Arnie, I need to ask you a few things," Turner said.

Arnie gave a small nod.

"You shot Jake an awful lot of times."

"He had offended Satan."

"Why'd you pick that warehouse to leave him in?"

"It was vacant."

"Why the third floor?" They'd found him on the second floor.

"I wouldn't be interrupted."

Turner resisted the urge to glance at Fenwick.

"Must have been tough carrying him up all those stairs."

"I don't remember."

"We still can't figure out where you hid your car so it couldn't be seen."

"In the alley."

"Why'd you take his underwear?"

Arnie turned his eyes on Turner. For the first time Turner thought he detected a semblance of recognition.

"Are you trying to trick me?"

"We didn't find his underwear."

"Yes."

"The boy this morning didn't have his underwear either."

"Yes."

"We need to look for it. Can you tell us where it is?"

"No. I don't remember."

For fifteen more minutes Turner questioned him. The more Turner asked, the worse Arnie's memory became. Finally Turner beckoned the lawyer and the parents out of the room. He leaned against the wall in the corridor. The parents looked anxious, the lawyer remained silent. Robsart, Fenwick, and the state's attorney looked on.

"He didn't do it," Turner said.

"Thank God," Mrs. Pantera said.

"He's in very bad shape," Turner said. "That glazed look."

"Are you a therapist, Mr. Turner?" Mr. Pantera asked.

Robsart stepped in. "Confessing to a murder and wasting the police's time like this is a serious criminal offense in itself. We need to talk."

She led them to her office. The lawyer stayed behind and said to Turner and Fenwick, "We've had trouble with Arnie for a long time. He's been hospitalized before for depression. I'll do what I can. Thank you for being understanding."

Back in the car, Fenwick said, "Add this to the fiasco list. How much time did we waste up here?"

"Too much."

"Have we ever met anybody that whacked out yet?"

"Remember the woman who lied about having borne six kids? Claimed it never happened. Or how about the guy with the beer truck in his living room?"

Fenwick laughed.

"And those were just since this summer. Need I go on?"

Halfway back to Area Ten, Turner found he could barely keep his eyes open.

"Don't fall asleep," Fenwick said.

"If we ever solve this, I'm going to sleep for a week."

At Area Ten they found the bedlam of reporters nearly nonexistent.

"What happened to all the media?" Fenwick asked the uniform working the front desk.

"Made a deal with the Commander. Regular morning and afternoon press conferences. Police personnel not to be harassed."

"Miracle," Fenwick said.

On the fourth floor, Blessing brought them over to the map and showed them the latest printout. "We've been making calls all day, following up the theory that it's a serial killer around the country murdering sports kids who've had articles about them in the paper. We have a total of eighteen such deaths in the past five years. We called local papers or police departments in every city in the country with a population over a hundred thousand, which meant over three hundred calls. We figured, or we hoped, they'd have anything in their own cities or a small town nearby."

"What about crushed testicles?"

"Most didn't know but said they'd try to find out."

"How's the pattern for places and dates?" Turner asked.

They strode over to the map. "See the yellow pins?"

The detectives nodded.

"All around the country," Blessing said. "And no longer in chronological or geographical order."

"Shit," Fenwick said.

"There's gotta be a pattern," Turner said.

Blessing said nothing.

"What about underwear?"

"Most didn't know, but said they were sure somebody would have remembered something like that. A few were honest and said nobody checked. Some of these were awful accidents where not just one kid got killed. Whatever they told me didn't add up to a pattern up here."

"I'm tired," Fenwick announced.

"Any news from Millwood?" Turner asked.

"Nothing so far. They're doing the same as you. Talking to the friends and relatives, schoolmates, neighbors, possible drug connections. They've got some guy coming up here later with all they get. We'll put it all on the computers. They've called almost every hour with updates."

Turner and Fenwick examined the printout carefully.

"You see any pattern?" Fenwick asked.

"Nothing," Turner said. "The only pattern that exists so far are the crushed-testicle cases."

Fenwick said, "Let's get the cities on these eighteen and match them with where everybody we've talked to lived in the past twenty years."

"That's incomplete," Blessing said. "I ran each through the computer for criminal records. The current driver's license information just gave us this state for addresses. We'd have to call all fifty states to check pasts on all of these. I'm getting Social Security records. So far the answer is none of these people lived in any of those cities at that time or in cities that were close to the killings."

"Except Waverly from Seattle to Spokane when he was in college," Turner said.

"So the killer visited," Fenwick said.

"If our theory is correct, somebody did. Problem is, what if the killer isn't one of the people we've talked to so far?"

"The killer has to know something of the pattern of these kids' lives."

"Maybe it's random chance. That's why there's no pattern. Killer passes through town. Looks in back issues of local newspapers for his victims. If in the time he's around, he sees his opportunity, they die."

"Assuming one of the people we've talked to is the killer, how could we track all these people for all those years? Even if we checked all the airlines for these people, they could have driven, gone by train. They could have lived halfway between two of the cities."

"Did somebody track them?"

"No."

"They could also have lived under a false name."

"That's doable but tough in our day of paper trails."

"Can we get credit-card records?"

"We can try."

"So what the hell do we have?" Fenwick asked.

Blessing looked at the latest computer printout. "This is all in the last ten years. We didn't put this morning's in yet. We have crushed testicles in five cities, counting Goldstein here. They are on random dates of the year, spaced irregularly through that time." He attached the printout to the corkboard.

Turner read out loud:

"April 5, 1985, in Spokane, Washington—supposed suicide, possible murder.

"October 23, 1986, in Fresno, California—gang killing.

"July 19, 1991, in Odessa, Texas—car accident.

"January 31, 1993, in St. Louis, Missouri—suicide."

"We have missing underwear here and in two other cities," Blessing said. "August 10, 1986, in Rapid City, South Dakota, and September 17, 1990, in Abilene, Texas."

Blessing pointed, "We have articles written about them and dead kids in seventeen places without Goldstein and Douglas."

"April 5, 1985, in Spokane, Washington, supposed suicide— possible murder.

"May 26, 1985, in Portland, Oregon—gang violence.

"June 17, 1985, in St. Paul, Minnesota—three kids in the same car accident. All had been featured in the same article so we counted all three.

"August 10, 1986, Rapid City, South Dakota—suicide.

"October 23, 1986, in Fresno, California—gang killing.

"November 1, 1986, in Padre Island, Texas—two kids in a swimming accident.

"February 1, 1987, Denver, Colorado—skiing accident.

"May 20, 1987, Cheyenne, Wyoming—suicide.

"March 21, 1988, Tucson, Arizona—car accident.

"September 17, 1990, in Abilene, Texas—four kids in a car; one had an article so we only count one.

"July 19, 1991, in Odessa, Texas—car accident.

"January 26, 1992, in Birmingham, Alabama—car accident.

"February 5, 1992, in Boulder, Colorado—shot by best friend.

"July 4, 1992, in Duluth, Minnesota—boating accident.

"July 5, 1992, in New Orleans, Louisiana—suicide.

"January 31, 1993, in St. Louis, Missouri—suicide."

"We've called all of these?" Turner asked.

166

"Spoke to cops and medical examiners in each city. Most were sympathetic."

They worked at trying to separate out the data, using different combinations and rearranging the information. When they finished, Turner looked at the results. "This tells me nothing," he said.

Fenwick handed him a list. "These are the accidents. Three of the eight are in Texas. I don't think that helps."

"If it is a very smart serial killer, he or she could have done some or all of these, made them look like suicides or accidents, or murders, or any goddamn thing."

"Where's what you've got on where everybody we've talked to lived?"

"Here," Blessing said.

"One of them lived in Texas from September 1980 to June 1985. During which time none of the killings happened in Texas. Waverly wasn't playing in any of these cities on the days of the killing. The list doesn't point to him as the killer. None of the others has lived in these cities during any of these times."

"What earthly good is this?" Fenwick asked.

"Maybe I was wrong," Turner said. His shoulders slumped. "I thought we had something."

"One curious thing," Blessing said. "We couldn't get any background on your Jose Martin or his dad. They have no history before four years ago. They appear in our records but not before that."

"No Social Security on Mr. Martin?" Turner asked.

"Not before four years ago," Blessing said.

"There's got to be Social Security records," Turner said.

"Not if they changed their identities. Not if they worked very hard at establishing a new life. What are they running from? Want me to hunt some more?"

"Yes, do what you can, but I'll ask myself," Turner said. "Call the cops who were outside their house and see if either of them left early this morning."

Minutes later the reply came back. Nothing unusual. Kid left for school under escort at the regular time. Father left for work fifteen minutes later. Both were in the house. Nobody came or went before then.

"That is still too odd," Turner said. "I'll be seeing the kid tonight at my place. If I have to, I'll drag him over to his dad's and get answers from both of them."

Joyce, the assistant, walked up to Blessing and handed him a note.

"This ought to cheer you guys up," Blessing said. "We just got a big anonymous tip, says here Daryl Logan, the representative from the university in the sky box, was with the boys after the game. Went with them to their car."

"We've had a confession, why not a fake lead?" Fenwick asked.

"I'm not putting a lot of hope into this," Turner said, "Caller isn't still on the line?" he asked Joyce.

"I tried to keep him talking, but he gave me the message and hung up."

"Did he sound old, young?"

"Nothing particular in the voice. No background noises that I remember."

"We recording the calls?"

"Yeah, we're tapped into the emergency system," Blessing said. "We've got everything. I'll get it for you."

"Does this justify our talking to the guy?" Turner asked.

"Better get a state's attorney and the Commander up here," Fenwick said. "We got no physical evidence on this."

"We'd never get a search warrant based on an anonymous tip," Turner said.

"Like to have a microscopist go over his car," Fenwick said.

Assuming the killer was bright enough to erase all fingerprints in the car that drove Goldstein to his place of death, then their next best bet was a microscopist. The microscopist could, as Sherlock Holmes suggested, find things out from the smallest detail. In this case the microscopist could go over the seats in Daryl Logan's vehicle. He or she could compare the minutest threads found in the car with Jake Goldstein's pants and jacket. If Goldstein had been in the car, a microscopist should find traces.

"Lots of immediate pressure on this one," Blessing said. "Should be able to shake something loose."

But half an hour later in the commander's office, Blessing's comment seemed essentially untrue.

"You have absolutely no physical evidence," the assistant state's attorney said. "You have no justification for a warrant of any kind. I don't see probable cause in an anonymous phone call. How many calls have you gotten? Probably hundreds, maybe thousands? Not one has led to a real break in the case, has it?"

Turner, Fenwick, and the commander shook their heads.

"You might be justified in talking to him, but I would be very careful."

Poindexter said, "You know the pressure we've been under on this case. You're in a political office. You know we've got to have something."

"But if you have no justification for a search or if you try something illegal and blow the case, it'll be worse. You know what the media will do if you announce you have a suspect or if you're even questioning someone. I still don't know how you avoided anything with that Waverly guy from the team."

"We were careful."

"Well, you'll have to be careful again."

Fenwick asked, "Do we call him and ask him, please, sir, to come in so we can chat, or do we find out where he lives and bust down his door?"

The assistant state's attorney did not smile. "Go talk to him at his house. Don't search for anything. Don't touch anything. Unless he's got a dead body hanging in the parlor, don't do anything."

Before they left, Blessing gave them a preliminary report on Logan's background. He'd lived all his life in the Chicago area.

Fenwick grumbled about "dead body in the parlor" for over half the drive from Area Ten to the Golden Ridge subdivision south of New Lenox in unincorporated Will County.

"This is going to be useless," Fenwick said.

"We've got to try," Turner said.

"What's the deal on Jose Martin and his dad?" Fenwick asked.

"I intend to find out," Turner said. "I'll have that answer before I go to bed tonight."

They took the Dan Ryan Expressway to Interstate 57, picked up Interstate 80 west, and exited at Maple Avenue in New Lenox. Using his *Chicago & Vicinity 6 County Street Finder,* Turner found Daryl Logan's address.

Some of the condos in the subdivision were half finished. Piles of wood and bricks surrounded a few of the structures. Immense clots of mud left by construction vehicles littered the street.

The light was on in Logan's condo. He answered their knock and looked quite surprised to see them. He led them into a sparsely furnished living room. He had only a black leather couch, an easy chair, and a compact-unit stereo system in it as furniture. No pictures hung from the wall. No bodies hung from the ceiling. Logan turned down a symphony playing on the stereo.

Turner said, "We need to check a number of things with you, Mr. Logan." The man wore a St. Basil's University sweatshirt, faded blue jeans, white socks, and running shoes. He didn't need a belt for the jeans to hug his narrow hips.

Turner thought, He's got enough of a build to carry around a struggling teenager, if he had to.

"I'm surprised you're here," Logan said.

"Someone told us the boys went back to the sky box after going to the locker room."

"Who told you that?" Logan asked.

"We received a call," Turner said. "It said you had gone to the car with the boys after the game."

"An anonymous call? This is an insult! After the game, I escorted the university's guests to their rented limousine and then went to my car and drove home. You can check with the guests about who went where. I can give you the list."

"Please," Turner said.

Logan stared at the cops for a half a minute. Finally he said, "I'll get it." He ascended stairs in the hallway and returned moments later. He handed Turner a list. "There are their home addresses. I can get you the numbers in the morning or I suppose directory assistance in their cities could get the numbers. You realize if you do that calling, people could begin to think I had some connection to this. I see no need for my reputation to be destroyed because you have been unable to come up with a suspect. If word of this gets out, my career at the university would be in jeopardy. And don't tell me that if I'm innocent, it can't hurt me. We've all seen what a media frenzy can do. If a whisper of this gets out, cameras will camp outside my door for days on end. Media people will attempt to talk to me, my family, and anyone who knows me."

Turner said, "I understand the media problem, Mr. Logan. We will do our best. You aren't a suspect. At the moment we just have some questions."

Turner and Fenwick asked their questions. Logan's answers gave them no cause to arrest him or treat him as a suspect and certainly gave them no excuse to go to a judge and ask for a warrant. They left after an hour.

Fenwick slammed his car door. "Into the fiasco column with another one."

The entire ride back to Area Ten passed in depressed silence.

Back on the third floor, Turner sat with his elbows on top of the desk and his head cupped in his hands. Fenwick plopped his bulk into his chair and swung his feet up onto his desk. He entwined his fingers and placed them behind his head. He stared at the ceiling.

"Is there much point to sitting here like this?" Fenwick asked.

"We're getting just as far doing this as we were running around the countryside."

"Did we eat lunch?"

"I thought we had something."

Commander Poindexter entered the room. They told him about their session with Logan.

After their conversation with the commander, Turner said,

"I'm going home to check on this Jose Martin thing. I'll probably grab a bite to eat."

"I'm going to stay here for a while and go over reports and statistics. Maybe something will leap out at me from our list of killings," Fenwick said.

"I'll be back in a couple hours at most. I'm going to try and keep this day to one that ends at midnight. We're at a big dead end. I don't need to ruin my health for this."

In the parking lot Turner saw Ian drive up in his green Range Rover. Turner climbed into the seat next to his friend.

"You look like hell," Ian said.

"I feel like it."

"Want to go for a drink?"

"No. I need to get home. We can talk here for a few minutes."

"What happened today?"

"More nothing. The creepiest kid on the planet confessed to the murder." Turner told him about his day.

"I'm sorry your idea didn't lead to something more concrete. If it is a serial killer working around the country, that's going to be tough to solve," Ian said.

"Yeah. I'm more worried about my kid. I've still got uniformed cops at the house. We won't be able to keep that long. My son and his buddy Jose are both there. Jose is the kid you were lusting after. Speaking of which. . . ." Turner told Ian about visiting the Martin home the night before.

Turner finished, "Plus, Blessing can only find identification for them from four years ago to now."

Ian said, "Tell me about the picture on the television again."

"It was just them smiling."

"No, the background."

"I don't know." Turner thought a minute. "It was just a crowd scene at a parade. Right behind them was a booth with a guy selling magazines and tapes, I think."

"Big guy at the table with one of those huge handlebar mustaches? Leather vest, no shirt underneath?"

"Yeah, maybe."

"That's Mrs. Sally, by day a chunky leather man, by night an overweight drag queen. He has a booth at every Gay Pride Parade in Chicago. He's not supposed to. The parade organizers and/or the police always chase him away."

"Why is this important for me to know?"

"The picture was taken at the Gay Pride Parade."

"Lots of people go to the Pride Parade who aren't gay."

"I didn't say they were gay."

"Would they have the nerve to live openly together if they weren't father and son?"

"Describe what you saw of Mr. Martin's tattoo," Ian commanded.

"I couldn't see it real well."

"Just tell me what you saw."

"Maybe the wing of a bird or a butterfly. The bottom half of a wheel. Why, is that the totem of a gay motorcycle group?"

Ian did not laugh. He said, "Two butterflies, the tips of their wings barely touching and then a motorcycle racing between them, is the symbol for a very sweet group of men who ride motorcycles. They also happen to be gay."

"Maybe Mr. Martin is gay and Jose is his straight son. It can happen, you know."

"I'd bet my baseball autographed by all of the 1969 Cubs that they are not father and son."

"I don't want to know that."

"Why not?"

"Because in the state of Illinois, police, schoolteachers, nurses, what-all, have to, by law, report any case of abuse they know about or suspect."

"This is abuse?"

"They've been living together since at least Jose's freshman year. He is still underage."

"You would turn them in?"

"The law says if a person who is aware of abuse doesn't report it and is caught not reporting it, he or she loses their job."

"You don't know their story. They may love each other. You can't simply turn them in." They were silent several moments.

"Brian's been Jose's best friend for more than three years."

Ian gazed at his friend. "Are you worried about Brian being gay?"

"No. You know the statistics. The kids of gay parents are as likely to be gay as the kids of straight parents."

"Are you worried that Jose and Brian might have had sex?"

"I don't know if I want to talk about that. I don't want to know the details of what my kid might have been doing. Lots of straight kids fool around in their early teens. If they didn't, your life would have been a lot different."

"Brian protecting Jose and Mr. Martin's secret means he understands, cares for them, has an open mind, doesn't get frightened by people who are different. Brian's a good kid. I think you can trust him. I wouldn't trade him for half the teenagers on the planet."

They sat in silence for a while. Finally Turner said, "I should get home."

Ian squeezed his knee. "If I can help, call me."

N I N E

At home, Paul found Jeff playing electronic games with Ben. Paul hugged his younger son and his lover.

"Got time for a game, Dad?"

"Maybe later. Is your homework done?"

"Yeah, we ate at Mrs. Talucci's. I like the police around the house. Mrs. Talucci made them come in and eat dinner with us. They were nice."

"I'm glad. Where's your brother?"

"Upstairs. They're studying for a test."

As Paul ascended the stairs, he didn't hear any sounds coming from his son's room. He tapped lightly on the door. He got a lazy "Yeah" in response.

He opened the door. Jose was sitting at his son's desk. He was staring at a page of a paperback copy of *Great Expectations*. Brian had a hand casually draped over his friend's shoulder while pointing with his other hand to a passage in the book.

"I told you it was Pip," Brian said.

"Okay, yeah."

Paul thought back to the numerous other times he'd seen his son and Jose having physical contact. Horsing around at the neighborhood pool. Wrestling, punching playfully, sitting next to each other on a couch with their legs and knees touching.

Jose turned to Paul and grinned. He said, "Hey, Mr. Turner. How's it going? Tough case you got. I like the protection when I go everywhere. I feel like the President with all the security guards."

"Jose, I need to talk to you," Paul said.

"Okay." Jose glanced at Brian. "Is something up?"

"He's my dad. He's a cop. He asks questions. He wanted to know about you and your dad, and I wouldn't tell him anything. I told him to ask you."

The two friends looked at each other. Jose nodded, then turned to Paul. Jose's smile was gone and his black eyes glittered.

"Did Brian know you wanted to talk to me?" Jose asked.

"Yes."

"And he didn't say anything to me about it?"

"He wouldn't tell me your secret. I asked him not to tell that I wanted to talk to you. Don't blame Brian."

"Okay, I guess," Jose said.

"That picture of you and your dad on the television set," Paul said. "That was taken at the Gay Pride Parade."

"This is bullshit," Jose said. His face was twisted in anger and his fists were clenched. He stood up. "I don't have to listen to this. You better talk to my dad."

"He's not your dad, is he?"

Fear chased all other reactions off Jose's face.

"Mr. Turner, what are you talking about? He's. . . ." Jose took a step toward Paul and tipped over the chair he'd been sitting in.

"There are no records of identification for you or Mr. Martin before four years ago. You both appear out of nowhere."

"That's not your business," Jose said.

"Jose," Paul said very quietly. "Please, sit down."

176

"Don't you try and wreck what we've got, Mr. Turner." A tear crossed Jose's right cheek. He brushed at it with the sleeve of his white sweatshirt.

"I just want to find out what's going on," Paul said.

"You're gonna screw everything up." Jose said this with quiet defeat.

"I want to help."

"You're gonna screw everything up!" Now the words were repeated with a trace of defiance. "I'm not going to let that happen," Jose said. Now he was angry and loud. "I'm not gonna let you or anybody ruin what I've got!"

"I don't want to ruin anything, Jose. Please, sit down."

Brian said, "He's my dad, Jose. You know you can trust him. He's okay. You've always trusted him. I have. You know I do."

Jose yanked the chair off the ground and straddled it backwards. He pointed a finger at Paul. "You don't have to ask me anything. I'm going to tell you. Nobody's gonna ruin what I got. Nobody. I'm going to tell, and we'll run if we have to. You can't stop us."

Paul said nothing to this angry frontal attack.

"Come on, Jose," Brian said. "It'll be okay."

"You should have warned me," Jose said.

Brian looked agonized. He gazed from his dad to his friend. "I kept your secret," he finally said.

"Big deal."

"Why don't you wait in the living room, Brian," Paul said.

"I don't care if he hears this," Jose said. "He knows most of it."

"Jose," Paul said, "I don't want to make trouble for you. I want to listen and understand."

Jose pulled in a deep breath, spread his arms wide on the back of the chair, and looked at Paul intently. His gaze seldom wavered from Paul's eyes as he told his story.

"I grew up to be a wild kid. My parents didn't know how to handle me, and after a while, they didn't want anything to do with me. They had problems of their own. I'd been placed in two different juvenile homes by the time I was nine. By age eleven I spent most of my time in foster homes and being passed around by state and city departments of child welfare. It wasn't in this state and Martin wasn't my last name, so you won't be able to trace me. The first time I had sex was with a thirteen-year-old in the basement of a child welfare center. I was ten. They had seventeen of us staying where there was supposed to be only five. He showed me how to hustle guys for money. Others showed me how to steal, sell drugs, live on the streets, and on my wits."

"I'm sorry," Paul said.

"I don't know if I want you to say anything, Mr. Turner. I've never told any adult besides Will all this. I think I'd just like to tell it."

Paul remained silent.

"No foster home could hold me. I ran away to somewhere warm and lived with a series of guys who were happy to keep me as long as I returned sexual favors. When I was twelve, I met Will. He didn't want to have sex with me. He was this nice gay man who lived next door to the guy who was keeping me. Will would do carpentry work out in his garage every night after he got home from work. I would go over there and watch and talk with him. I offered myself to him. He said no. He showed me how to carve, measure, hammer, and put things together. I'd screw my sugar daddy at night and run around on the streets all day, then spend an hour or so with Will after he got home.

"My sugar daddy got tired of me. I was too wild. I wouldn't settle down even for a safe roof over my head. Then I got in trouble with the cops again. They sent me to another foster home, but I ran away the first night. On my thirteenth birthday I used a gun to rob somebody. The cops were after me. I ran to Will. He said I'd have to turn myself in. I said I would if I could live with him. He told me that no one would sanction a gay man just bringing a kid into his home. He was afraid of the law. I did turn myself in. I got sent to a juvenile place for six months. While I was there, I thought about Will a lot. He could be gruff, but he always took time to explain things to me. I'd had enough of chaos. I wanted the calm life he had. In that juvenile home I had time to think and plan.

"They let me out in the care of another foster family. The first day I went over to Will's. He seemed surprised and happy to see me. I told him I wanted to live with him and everything. He said no. I tried every seduction technique I'd learned. He told me he'd let me come over after school and do my homework and he'd work with me every day and we'd see if we got along. I knew I had him. I did everything I promised. The foster family didn't mind where I went. The cops weren't over all the time hassling them or me. I began staying longer and longer at Will's each day. We started eating dinner together. He showed me how to cook."

Jose's eyes got shiny. "That Christmas I gave him a gift that I'd carved from a block of wood. On Christmas Eve I asked if I could stay late. He agreed. He made a big fire in his fireplace. He let me snuggle up to him. We watched some of those old weepy Christmas movies together. At midnight I kissed him for the first time. I wanted to live with him from then on. He wouldn't let me. Finally the next summer, after I graduated eighth grade, we decided to move out of that town to Chicago. No one knew us here. We could change our identities and pose as father and son. The foster family wouldn't miss me. I love him more than anything. I will never do anything to hurt him. If you try and take us to court or report us, I'll never testify against him. I'll deny everything I've told you. I'll run away. I can live on my own. Now that I'm older I can do even more than when I was a kid."

Tears ran down Jose's face. "Don't wreck it for me, for us, Mr. Turner. I know you're a cop and there's rules about what you're supposed to do, but I swear to God, this is the best thing that has ever happened to me. We're not hurting anybody. Please let us be."

By any standard this was an older man living in a sexual relationship with a minor. It was illegal and Paul Turner could lose his job if he didn't report it. He did not want to let his career rest on the possibility that no one would ever find out that he knew these two were directly violating the law.

"Everything will work out," Paul said. "My goal as a cop and a person is not to wreck somebody's life. I need to think about this and probably talk to Will. And don't be mad at Brian. He's a good and loyal friend. He did extraordinarily well in a tough situation."

"Okay." Jose wiped his eyes with the back of his hand.

"I'll drive you home in a little while," Paul said. As he left the room, he heard the voices of the two teenagers, but did not stop to listen. Several minutes later Brian came down the stairs. Paul met him in the kitchen.

"What's going to happen?" Brian asked. "Are you going to report them?"

"Relax," Paul said. "I'm not going to make any hasty decisions or do something to hurt your friend. You were in a tough spot. You did a good job."

"I still feel kind of strange."

"Did Jose say he was angry at you?"

"No, he's cool."

"When did he tell you he was gay?" Paul asked.

"He didn't have to. I went over there to play one time just after he moved here. As I walked up to the front door, I happened to see them kiss. Jose saw me watching. I already knew about gay stuff because you'd talked to me. I just figured it was another gay thing. Never thought a lot about it. He told me the whole story last summer when we went on that weekend camping trip."

Paul heard a knock on the front door. Jeff answered and a minute later Rose Talucci entered the kitchen with an iron kettle. "I've got leftover ravioli from when the boys ate. Want me to fix it? You look awful."

Brian left the kitchen.

Paul talked about the case as he cut vegetables for salad, heated bread, and set the table while Mrs. Talucci warmed up the home-made ravioli. Halfway through dinner he finished the story of the case.

"I'll talk to my sources about protection for the boys," Mrs. Talucci said. "You won't have to worry." Her "talking to peo-ple" could mean anything from being connected to the most powerful Mafia don in the country to gossiping with the neighbors. Often amazing things seemed to get done when Mrs. Talucci talked to people.

"That's not all that's bothering you," Mrs. Talucci said.

"Sometimes I wish you weren't quite so shrewd, Rose," Paul said.

"How can I help?"

He told her about Jose and Will. Mrs. Talucci listened without interrupting.

Paul finished, "If I don't tell and it ever comes out, I'm in trouble. Doubly so because I'm a gay cop. It looks like I'm trying to cover up a man-boy relationship, and I am. Ian said I shouldn't turn them in. Brian doesn't want me to hurt his friend. He's watching me carefully on this. It's a hell of a dilemma. He looks to me to do the right thing. I don't know what that is in this case. Rose, I don't know what to do."

Rose sipped her tea and sighed. "It is not as much of a dilemma as you think," she said. "When is the boy going to be eighteen?"

"In five months."

"In which case it is not a problem for anyone anymore."

"Unless Jose gets angry and turns on him, wants to sue him. There are statutes of limitation on the criminal laws, but he could sue him for years after."

Rose sat thoughtfully for a few minutes, then reached over and patted Paul's arm. "These two people love each other. Jose is no longer a problem to society. In fact he is very productive. He works hard in school. Gets good grades. Hangs around with good kids like Brian. He doesn't do drugs. He left behind a life of hell." She sighed deeply. "I will be ninety-three years old in two weeks. I have seen a lot of pain and agony in those years and a lot of joy and happiness. Now I'm dying. I know people put each other through hell often for no other reason than that they exist. Who is to judge that Jose and Will don't truly love each other? I suppose twenty, even ten, years ago I might have thought differently. Maybe knowing that I'm going to die, thinking about it, makes me see things in new ways. I see two human beings who have found caring and love. Who has been harmed? The boy? He's been in your home hundreds of times. Is he a bad influence? Do you like him? Is he going to be a good adult? Is telling about them going to make either of them better?"

Paul shook his head no.

"It is wrong for adults to exploit kids for sex. Is this situation that?"

"No," Paul said.

"The question is not society's morals. On one hand you've got moral rigidity; on the other, common sense and doing the right thing. The possibility of leaving them be and it affecting your job is incredibly remote. Your job is also to ensure crime doesn't happen. Because of this relationship, Jose has stopped committing crimes. I think you should leave them be. They've found love. Let them keep it. It's not up to you to destroy it. Trust a dying old woman one more time, Paul. It is okay if you don't tell. Be thankful he's not out trying to get revenge on everyone who hurt him since he was small. The list would never end."

They talked quietly for a few minutes before Rose left. Paul hugged Ben and Jeff. Then he drove Jose home.

In the car Jose was quiet. As they pulled up in front of his house, Jose asked, "Are you going to talk to Will?"

"Not tonight," Paul said. "You and Mr. Martin have nothing to fear from me."

"Thanks, Mr. Turner," Jose said.

Paul stuck out his hand. Jose shook it. Paul saw the uniformed cops sitting in their car. He watched Jose enter the house. The uniformed cops weren't going to be able to stay on guard long. They had to solve the case soon.

At Area Ten headquarters Turner found Fenwick sitting at the table next to the corkboard on the fourth floor. Remnants of a deep-dish pizza from Uno's lay on the floor near Fenwick's feet. Fenwick's shirt was open and his tie was undone. He had red tomato sauce on his shirt and on the paper he was reading.

"You took your time," Fenwick said.

Turner told him what he'd learned. He finished, "So Jose and Mr. Martin are out. I think we've got a serial killer on our hands. We aren't going to be one of those police departments that refuses to acknowledge we have a serial killer because we're afraid of frightening the public. I think this is a very smart serial killer. But he or she had to start sometime. And judging from the three area killings we've got, this is a very angry person."

"And so?"

"Something Rose said when she was talking made sense. The killer is getting even for all the wrongs the world has done to him."

"And so, Mr. Psychology Professor?"

"And so it started when the person was young. Isn't that in the profiles? It starts from when they were kids. Blessing had that stuff where people lived. How far did he go back?"

"I don't know."

They trooped over to Blessing's desk. Turner saw more remnants of pizza around Blessing's computer.

"I went back as far as I could on anyone who'd been talked to by any officer or detective on the case."

"What if the killer isn't one of the people we've already talked to?" Fenwick asked. "In fact that's pretty likely, isn't it?"

Blessing said, "We could try going through all the people you haven't talked to. Did you want the entire planet covered or just this continent?"

Fenwick was silent. Blessing said, "I got Social Security to give me most of it."

"Wouldn't they have addresses only from places people worked?"

"Yeah."

"How about before that? Can you find out where they came from originally?"

"You mean as kids?"

"Yeah, I guess."

Blessing gazed at the pages of names he'd been given. "Like I said earlier, I can try going through driver's license records, but I'd have to do it by state and ask the officials to check each person in each state."

"Why not start with the last address Social Security gave you? Start in that state for that person."

"It'll work, provided they didn't move and they were in a job that paid into Social Security, and then try and talk to someone who would have birth records, if they're computerized."

"Start with Illinois," Turner suggested. "Most of those on the list are probably from here. None of the killings were in Illinois until now. The killer started someplace else. So he lived someplace else. Illinois should be easiest. Finish it and then do the rest."

Fenwick asked, "What if the killer is smart enough to always kill where he doesn't live?"

"We've got to start someplace," Turner said. "Besides, the last three were here. So he doesn't live here?"

"This is getting kind of complicated," Fenwick said.

"Can you do it?" Turner said to Blessing. "We'll help."

"We can do it," Blessing said. "You've got pictures to look at."

"Do what?" Fenwick asked.

"From the funeral and the game," Blessing said. "I sent people over to the United Center and got copies of the tapes from all the cameras. Friends of mine in the Crime Lab put together all the crowd shots. You should go over them to see if you recognize anybody. I've got a television and a VCR set up back in the conference room. You can go over the funeral tapes at the same time."

"Golly, gee whiz, thanks," Fenwick said. "I didn't have anything else to do tonight. Are you ever inefficient?"

"No," Blessing said.

The crowd shots of the game were mercifully few. Cameras were supposed to concentrate on the action on the floor. After half an hour Turner said, "Look at this from the second half." He pointed the remote control at the screen and froze a frame. "Look, you can see Ben behind the bench but not Brian." He hit the button that moved the picture one frame at a time. "These aren't continuous, because the camera wasn't on them all the time. Look at this one. Ben is gone."

"One of the seats four rows above them is empty," Fenwick said.

Turner sent the frames backward and forward. "I can't make out a face."

"Me neither, but that seat is filled when Ben is there but not after he's gone."

They checked back through the tapes but this was the only section where the anomaly appeared.

"Could have been somebody going to the john?" Fenwick said.

"Could have been the killer," Turner said.

"Those seats are sold out well in advance. How could the killer get one?"

Turner shook his head.

They began running through the funeral tapes. Three quarters of the way through the first one, Fenwick said, "Hold it. Run it back. There." The camera had caught a man in a security uniform with long hair and a drooping mustache just turning away. "Isn't that the kind of guy Brian described?"

"Yes," Turner said.

"Looks fake," Fenwick said. "Got to be a disguise."

"Not very tall," Turner said. "Can't really tell, is he sort of chunky?"

"Waverly is tall. So is Logan. Riley is maybe that short. He's more muscular. You can't see much of the body. Certainly can't identify anything from this. Maybe we can have it blown up. Some scar or something might show up."

"In our dreams."

Just before midnight they checked with Blessing on what he had found.

"Most are from Illinois," the computer expert said. "Saved us a lot of time."

"Who's from out of state?" Turner asked.

Blessing handed him a list of seventeen names.

"Where's the list of deaths?" Turner asked.

Fenwick rummaged on the large table and brought it to Turner.

The three of them gazed down the list. Turner pointed. "Drew Riley got his driver's license in Spokane, Washington, in 1978."

"That was seven years before the killing there," Fenwick said.

"He live in our crushed-testicles cities?" Turner asked.

Blessing looked. "Nope. Not in the underwear cities either."

"Anybody else on the list match anywhere?" Turner asked.

They looked and shook their heads.

"We have one very tenuous connection," Fenwick said. "That does not a killer make."

"He works across the street from where we found the body. It would be handy for him."

"Millwood is not handy for him."

"Wait," Blessing said. He checked a printout. "I have absolutely no addresses for Riley after 1985."

"Sounds odd to me."

"Yeah. I was matching addresses we do have. We don't have any for him."

"Why not?"

"He didn't pay Social Security."

"Can you do that?"

"Sure. If you've got a job that has a private pension fund. Not that odd. Hell, many of the teachers in Illinois don't pay Social Security. They have the Teacher's Retirement System they pay into."

"So it could mean nothing."

"But it is odd."

"Odd and worth checking?" Fenwick asked. "Being sort of the size of the guy who gave Brian the note and who appeared on the funeral tape is not what I want to bring to a boss."

"Do we talk to him again?" Turner asked.

"We could get the Commander and the Assistant State's Attorney back in here. You want to be the one to tell them we're going to question a witness based on this kind of connection?"

"Riley works late. I bet he's still there," Turner said. "Maybe I'll stop by on my way home."

Blessing and Fenwick shook their heads.

"I won't screw up the case," Turner said.

"I'm going with," Fenwick said.

"No need."

"Right. After we find you sliced up and dead and the Commander asks me why I didn't go with you to confront a possible deadly killer, I'll just say, 'Paul said I didn't need to.'"

They drove to the Lumber Street address. Even fewer street lights were working. Turner didn't see a car in front of the new health club, but he remembered that Riley had a hidden parking place. He saw a light in the upper room in front. Turner knocked loudly.

No one answered. A gust of wind chilled him as he stood uncertainly in front of the closed door. He banged louder.

Fenwick tapped him on the shoulder. "Look." Fenwick pointed across the street to the warehouse. "Isn't that lights on the third floor?"

Turner gazed at the darkened structure. "I'm not sure."

"I better check it out. I'll call for back-up on the way. I'll be right back." Fenwick trotted toward the car. The door behind Turner suddenly swung open.

Drew Riley's gold eyes gazed out at him inquisitively. "Detective. Sorry, I was in the john. Took me a while to get down here." He invited him in.

They climbed to the second story. Here newly delivered exercise machines sat, some half out of their boxes. A few were assembled. Drew perched on the seat of one machine and Turner took one across from him. Around them buckets, paintbrushes, tools, and cleaning rags littered the floor. Turner noted that he was painting bold stripes around the walls, alternating primary colors.

"This is going to be the exercise-machine room," Riley said. He fiddled with a large brush half covered with red paint. The sitting position pushed Riley's crotch into an even more prominent view than he'd noticed the first time. Turner glanced away.

"We had another murder," Turner said.

"In Millwood," Riley said.

"Yeah. Not very pleasant. We've got a very angry person on our hands."

"I work out my anger."

"You grew up in Spokane, Washington."

Riley gazed at him without changing expression. "You must have looked very hard to find that."

"Simple police work. We went back on everybody. You're the only one with a dead teenager in a city you came from."

"Oh."

"I couldn't find anybody else with a connection like that, only you."

"And that means?"

Turner shut his eyes and listened to the silence of the building. He could barely hear Riley's breathing as he sat there. No sounds penetrated to this room from outside. He wondered if back-up had arrived, if Fenwick would find anything across the street, and when he would knock on the door downstairs. Turner opened his eyes. He looked at the two metallic arms that stretched out from the machine at the height of his shoulders. "Killing in Millwood was one of the worst I've ever seen. Took this athlete and ripped him apart. Tore great strips of flesh and muscle off the frame."

"Awful."

"Where'd you live after Texas? We don't have an address for you since 1985."

"I inherited money from my uncle. I told you that the first time you talked to me. Mostly I bummed around. Lived here and there."

"No need to pay taxes or Social Security if you're living on an inheritance. Where'd you live?"

"You've looked up everything else. You can't find that?"

"You can save me a bunch of time running it through our computer system."

"I kind of lived everywhere."

"Three suspicious deaths in Texas in the past nine years involving kids who had their names in the papers as sports heroes."

"Sports heroes dying?"

"You play sports when you were a kid?"

"Didn't get into working out until after college."

"Why'd you take a job at the health club?"

"Why not? I enjoy it."

"We've done a lot of computer checking," Turner said. "Tomorrow we're going to go through the credit-card files of everyone we've talked to. We want to see if they were in any of the cities or on the way to or from the cities where any of these athletes died."

"You got lots of these cities?"

"Eighteen in the last nine years. We'll have the movements of everybody we talked to outlined and listed before the week is out. We'll track them on this huge chart on the wall. We've got floor-to-ceiling corkboard. We'll be able to surround each murder with the movements of all the people we've talked to."

"Hard to find out things after all this time."

"We'll talk to airlines and trains. Any credit-card transactions."

"Person could use cash."

"And bank withdrawals for days and weeks beforehand. We can get bank records that'll give us dates. We'll concentrate on sports kids who had articles written about them; the ones with testicles crushed, or with their underwear missing."

"Missing underwear? Sick."

"We'll also be blowing up frames from the tapes of the funeral and the crowd at last night's basketball game. The killer may have disguised himself, but we'll find something in the blow-ups that gives him away."

"You'll never catch the killer."

"I imagine we will. People can't move totally undetected in a computer-driven society."

189

"Take you a while to check all those computer records."

"We've got a huge task force. Won't take but a day or two."

They gazed at each other.

"Why are you here?" Riley asked.

"Told you. The connection with Spokane."

Riley nodded.

"And Texas. And no addresses."

"None of which is illegal." Riley smiled. "And now you come to my home to see if I hurry up and pack to get out of town."

"Are you planning to leave town? I wouldn't. We're going to get the killer whether from credit-card records or pictures."

"Yes." Riley was silent for a long time. "It sounds like you will." He ran his hand along the metal arm of the machine.

"Where were you this morning?" Turner asked.

Riley did not laugh maniacally or sneer or bluster or snarl or twist his face in rage. Nor did he stand up and scream, "You'll never catch me, copper." He did not make boasts about how clever he had been. Instead, he whipped the paintbrush he'd been fiddling with at Turner's head, and then lunged at him.

Turner banged his head onto one of the arms of the machine as he ducked. He felt droplets of paint on the right side of his face. As Riley dove into him, the machine tilted wildly and crashed to the floor. Entangled in the machine, Turner couldn't get his footing or balance, but it prevented Riley from getting a good grip on him.

Riley stepped back and aimed a kick at Turner's nuts. He missed but caught enough of his midsection to cause Turner to double over.

Riley dashed to a pile of weights a few feet away. Turner tried to grab his gun, catch his breath, and get out from the machine.

Riley picked up the heavy metal pole that had no weights on the ends. He charged toward Turner holding the pole like a lance.

Turner thrust himself from the machine seconds before the blunt end of the weight would have crashed into his skull. Riley rushed after Turner using the weight as if it were a quarterstaff, shoving Turner backward and keeping him off balance.

Turner managed to get both hands on one end of the weight and push Riley back for a moment, but the health instructor was in excellent shape, and Turner found himself giving ground.

Turner suddenly let go, rolled under the iron staff, and kicked his legs toward Riley, catching him a solid blow on his left knee. Riley staggered, tipped over a bucket of orange paint, drove the left end of the weight bar into the floor to keep himself from falling.

Turner thought he heard pounding on the door downstairs. Riley abruptly lifted his head to listen and banged his right temple against an out-thrust hand grip. Turner leaped at him. The couple of seconds he was dazed gave Turner time to handcuff Riley to one of the machines.

Breathing heavily, Riley tried to break the hold the cuffs had on him. Turner moved slowly back, watching Riley drag the machine halfway across the room. Turner had his gun out and trained on his prisoner when Fenwick popped his head in the door.

When the back-up arrived downstairs, they assigned them to keep everybody out except the commander and the state's attorney, both of whom showed up in less than half an hour. In that time Turner and Fenwick touched as little as possible and talked with Riley not at all except to read him his rights. The two detectives were determined not to taint any possible evidence or to screw up the paperwork process.

The swirl of the next few hours' activity was finally followed by a quiet moment in the interrogation room at the station. Riley and his attorney sat with Turner and Fenwick as the first hints of dawn rose over the lake. No one had spoken for a while after Turner had asked the simple question, Why?

Riley rubbed his hand slowly across the bruise on his forehead. He sighed. "Will you listen?"

Turner nodded.

Riley nodded as his lawyer repeated his warnings about incriminating himself. He told his story. "I grew up wild as a kid. Nobody could do anything with me. I kept an army of social workers busy. I sold more drugs in third grade than most dealers do in a lifetime. Twice, older kids almost killed me. I got beaten up by half the adults who tried to control me. I learned to fight. I was a small kid but I was so tough that nobody got into my butt in any of those homes. I learned about sex, but girls weren't too interested in a shrimpy little hoodlum. I sat in some corner and beat off looking at *Playboy* magazines.

"So I was living with this out-of-it older couple for a few months. I was just sixteen, but still in ninth grade, when I screwed up a drug deal with a guy on the high school football team. He decided to get revenge. One of the high school cheerleaders asked me out. Most popular and beautiful girl at the high school. I was stupid. I never figured out why she asked me. I was in a haze for days before the big date. She picked me up in her car. I was so proud of myself. I never had many dates with girls. Hell, I had few friends male or female. Mostly I had fights. I was a secretive, nerdy criminal.

"The date was perfect. We went to dinner and a dance, and afterwards she drove us out to Lover's Lane. I had an erection all the way out there. I couldn't believe my luck. When she had the car parked, I sort of reached over. She laughed and the passenger side door opened. It was her boyfriend who I'd screwed over. His buddies from the team were there too. I think originally they were just going to scare me. But it got out of hand. They tickled me. They took my clothes. I started crying and they laughed harder. I started hitting the nearest one. He was a big star on the basketball team. He tried to hold my arms. But I kicked and screamed. Things got ugly."

Riley shook his head. "They raped me. Over and over. I never reported it to anyone. Telling would have made it worse. I wasn't sure who all of them were or who fucked me. I thought I was going to die because I shit blood for days. That night as I crawled home without my clothes, I vowed I'd get revenge. I couldn't

192

then; I was too screwed up. But I formed a plan to get even. I changed. I got off drugs. I studied in high school. I had to be smarter than them.

"It took me five years to get through college. I tried dating a few girls, but I found I couldn't perform unless I got violent. All those years I worked out and planned. I thought about getting revenge on those who attacked me. I went back to Spokane and they were all fat and old. The guy who started it had been killed in a drug deal. None of them had an athletic career. Killing them would mean nothing. I figured I could even the score on high school stud athletes. First I tried robbing them, or wrecking their cars, even making obscene calls, minor stuff, then one time things got out of hand and I killed one. That night I went to a bar, got a girl, went home, and found I could perform with no problem. Two nights later I couldn't get it up. Figured it out. I could have sex as long as I killed some stud motherfucker first. I decided to get revenge on everyone who hurt me in my life, maybe not the real people, but stud athletes were in large supply."

Turner got done with the major parts of the paperwork just before the ten o'clock press conference. He and Fenwick glanced in mirrors in the john before they went out. Neither decided to clean up much. Let them see tired, hardworking cops.

They evaded the sillier questions, answered as much as they could of the more sensible, and let the commander handle most of the PR problems.

When Paul got home, the house was quiet. The boys were at school. He'd been up all night, but he was too keyed up to try and begin catching up on his sleep. He changed into jeans and a sweater and threw on a jacket. The wind was out of the north and howling. The first flurries of winter were predicted for that afternoon. He stopped at Rose's. He found her on the phone complaining to the alderman about potholes on the street.

After Rose hung up, she patted his arm, insisted he eat a meal, and let him tell her as much as he wanted about the case. After half an hour she insisted he go see Ben. Paul had planned to do this anyway.

He walked down to Ben's service station. As he passed Jennie's flower shop, he stepped in for a minute and picked up a dozen daffodils and a dozen red roses.

Outside the shop, Myra was bent over a small car. He heard bangs from the engine. She looked up, saw him, smiled, and straightened up. "Heard you were on television. Congratulations. Boss is in the back, whistling. You must make him happy." She noted the flowers. "Excellent touch. I like it when you follow my advice. He's in his office."

Paul made his way to the back. He found Ben peering at a computer screen. In one grease-covered hand he had a stack of bills, in the other a black felt-tip pen. Ben looked up from his work and smiled at Paul.

The flowers almost got crushed between them as they embraced. Paul felt one of Ben's hands stray from his back to the door. It shut with a thump. They held each other tightly and kissed passionately.